Pratima Mitchell was born in India and attended universities in Delhi, London and the US. She comes from a family of writers and was first published at the age of eleven. She has worked as a journalist, editor, waitress and teacher. She lives in Oxford, where she digs an allotment, rides her bike, plays the melodeon and writes in her garden shed. Her only daughter is a concert violinist.

indian summer

Pratima Mitchell

WALKER BOOKS

First published in Great Britain 2009 by Walker Books Ltd
87 Vauxhall Walk, London SE11 5HJ

2 4 6 8 10 9 7 5 3 1

Text © 2009 by Pratima Mitchell

Cover photographs: © 2009 Creatas/Photolibrary (Girl in sari);
© 2009 Alan Frank/Photolibrary (Girl in vest);
© 2009 Beren Patterson/Alamy (Landscape)

This book has been typeset in Baskerville.

Printed and bound in Great Britain by Clays Ltd, St Ives plc

British Library Cataloguing in Publication Data:
a catalogue record for this book is
available from the British Library

ISBN 978-1-4063-0817-4

www.walker.co.uk

For Rowena Akinyemi

A daughter is a disappointment. If you bring a daughter into this world, you have to be forgiven.

– Louise Bourgeois, Artist, 1911

To have a girl is to plant a seed in someone else's garden
– Hindi saying

Daughters aren't wanted in India...
– *Guardian* report 27 February 2007

One

One

SARLA

Ma can do anything: dissect plugs and make them work, change a tyre, run for cover under gunfire, parachute jump, water-ski, drive a lorry, type news reports as fast as she thinks. Multiplying double numbers in her head is as easy as turning perfect cartwheels … honestly, I'm not exaggerating; the list is endless. She's not too bad for thirty-something either. No plastic surgery, highlights … yet. It's all go. When she moves sparks fly. A bit like watching Wimbledon – *thwack, thwack, thwack, smash!*

My feelings about Ma are complicated. I swing from irritation to pride to concern. The other day her sister, my aunt Piloo, confided in her whispery anxious way that Ma's energy field was heading into terminator mode. "Her chakras are blocked!"

I laughed, because it was so typically Piloo, but it

was also worrying. I don't want Ma to be cut down in her prime. Piloo even bought her an appointment with her own homeopath as a birthday present. Piloo is into "alternative" in a big, big way: she gets her feet tickled (reflexology), her spine straightened (chiropractic), her skull massaged (sacro-cranial therapy), her body balanced (kinesiology). Things you wouldn't believe! Her life is full of yoga, chanting, energy healing, dervish dancing and astrology.

But (to go back to Ma) in my opinion the basic problem with superwoman is that in her view housekeeping is for an inferior species. She can't cook to save her life. It's possible that I'll go down in history as the biggest consumer of stir-fry, lamb pasanda, chicken kiev and all that crap that passes for proper food.

My best friend Grania said admiringly that Ma is Awesome and Dashing, A and D. We play this game sometimes when everyone gets labelled, like Gluglug Harry (her alcoholic uncle), VeeVee (Vicious Vixen, a.k.a. Valerie Vaz, our English teacher) or PiteeMee (so-sad Asmat in our class who looks permanently rained on). It makes us feel so superior, squashing people with our witty asides. Elizabeth (my other best friend) doesn't approve at all.

One Saturday morning in July, Ma was dashing around our Bayswater flat, *clip-clip-clip*, in heelless slippers, with her long black hair, wet as seaweed, flapping. One call ended and another would begin, because, wouldn't you know it, she is sooo popular and knows everybody. Then the doorbell went, *prinnnnng*, and *clip-clip-clip* she ran to answer it.

I heard, "OOOOH!" somewhat muffled by a gigantic bunch of red roses that hid her face. "Aren't they gorgeous?" she simpered, with a sickeningly coy look, though I bet they were just about as smelly as Simple soap and five minutes later their necks would collapse like dead geese.

"Lover boy Desmond?" I asked in an evil nasal drawl, smoothing a Häagen-Dazs choc-ice with almond coating between my lips. Ma gets really annoyed that I am so lumpy and un-chic. I hadn't bothered telling her this was my Last Treat, so I was giving it proper respect. I'm into rituals, and this was to be the last of unhealthy breakfasts. After this I was all sorted out on a diet of carrot sticks, celery and apples, because Grania and I were getting ready for the summer. We were going to be as lithe and slim and toned as the toothpicks in *Looks* magazine. All that toxic sludge would be flushed out. Mars bars, crisps and ice-cream wouldn't get a look-in.

There is another problem with Ma. She falls in love like a seal falling into water. Desmond was her latest flame. He was an American banker, firm-jawed, perma-tanned etc. etc. He sent flowers every Saturday and would appear on the doorstep cradling a bottle of champagne and looking lovesick. Creep.

"Oh, Poochi, what to do what to do?"

This was straight from the official phrase book of her old school, the Convent of the Immaculate Conception, Daroga, India. She slips into Indotalk when she's stressed. But she wasn't asking for advice, just being rhetorical like VeeVee when she rolls her eyes and splutters, "Ye Gods, what have we here?"

Whattodowhattodo? The phone rang again.

"Hello," she sang in her extra-charming voice, thinking it was Desmond asking if the roses had been delivered.

"Oh, *hello, Andrew!* She dropped into business mode. "WHA-AAT? DAMMIT! Just my luck...!" Then her hand snaked round the door for the knob (the other knob had fallen off) to shut it so I wouldn't eavesdrop.

My right leg was asleep with the effort of eating the ice-cream, so I shifted my weight to get more comfy and, from habit, glanced at Viktor's cage. I hadn't cleaned it since he'd died of geriatric complications more than two months ago; bits of straw snaggled through the bars. Viktor, oh, Viktor, I remembered and a lump came into my throat.

Viktor had been my friend for years. Suddenly there were tears in my eyes. Viktor's eyes never blinked and I could always see a tiny reflection of myself when I went up close to him.

I craned round to look in the mirror. A really depressing sight greeted me: not a cheekbone to be seen. People say I have intelligent eyes; black, maybe even brilliant, but *intelligent*? What does that mean? Now they were swimming like a tragic heroine and then I saw that the choc-ice had dripped all over the pale blue Bokhara rug. I swore. It was the nicest thing in our flat and Rita (Ma) had brought it back from one of her assignments in Central Asia.

That was when I'd stayed with New Agey Aunt Piloo. She's a social worker in Tower Hamlets and she isn't a bit like her sister − not in looks, temperament, style, nothing. Her face is pale, egg-shaped with a sucked-lemon expression. She plaits her hair in a long pigtail and follows a repulsive guru whose photo is on her bedside table. How can she open her eyes on him first thing in the morning? He has unattractive, crocodiley skin, eyes like fried eggs and garlands of spare tyres round his fat neck. Piloo's tried hard to get me interested in this guru stuff by telling me about his "miracles" – making flowers and Rolexes appear out of thin air, healing people from cancer and polio – all rubbish of course. Rita thinks she needs a man in her life.

Rita was still yakking on the phone, so I sniffed back my runny nose (she hates me doing that because it reminds her of people hawking up phlegm in India) and tried to work out a plan for the day. It was the last weekend before the summer holidays, so I was flexing my vegging-out muscles. Grania and Elizabeth were going away, but Rita and I had planned a windsurfing fortnight in Brittany. Afterwards we were heading for Paris, where Desmond was going to join us.

The light was taking on the low wattage greeny glow from the lime tree just outside the window. A rumble of thunder vibrated as the kitchen grew darker and greener like the inside of a huge glass bottle planted with ferns. Just for a second it was like the bottom of the sea in there, mysterious, threatening and full of unknown secrets.

We had so much junk: red and blue Indian hand-blocked curtains, terracotta toys, brass animals, tribal rugs, a dusty, messy mishmash. Nothing was ever cleared up because we didn't throw anything away; not a bit like Elizabeth's flat, which sparkled (they even polished their taps with a special tap polish!).

Ours was mixed-up, English and Indian, a bit like me.

As soon as she came back into the kitchen I knew something awful had happened. I tried to strobe-gaze her, but she wouldn't meet my eye. She shuffled around in a shifty way, scrunching her hair into a chignon with a biro, took out her secret cache of cigarettes hidden in a teapot and lit up.

"Ho ho ho, you've quit smoking, Reeda?" I drawled in American. I found it weirdly exotic how Desmond ended every sentence with a question mark.

She obediently ground out the coffin nail in the plughole of the sink. She kicked a kitchen chair, plonked herself down head in hands and groaned loudly.

"Whattodowhattodooo? Bad news, Poochi. That was Andrew from the office. They're sending me to Tarekstan. The bombing's started again. Jane's flying back because her father's dying in hospital. No one else is around."

It took a few seconds for the rush of information to filter into my brain, and then I realized what it meant. I shrieked, "So what about our holiday? What am I supposed to do all summer?"

She chewed a stray bit of damp hair looking, I was pleased to see, pretty mortified. I carried on shouting and yelling, though I should have known better than to make a scene. I should have been cool and sensible and understanding and tried to soothe her guilty conscience, which was staring me in the face like a cartoon spook. It wasn't new. My mum was a star television reporter, a single parent and her career was very important to her. She'd slogged out her guts to get to where she was. After all, she'd left my dad because she was so single-minded about work. But it never felt good coming second to her job.

My eyes landed on the plates stashed like a house of cards on top of the sink and I dug my nails into my palms to stop myself going over and sweeping them to the floor. One bit of me wanted to punish her and make her suffer.

Usually if she skips off on a reporting emergency her friends, or Piloo, or one of my friends rally round and have me to stay. But the timing was really bad – Elizabeth was all booked to go on a walking holiday in Austria with her family and Grania was going to her uncle's place in Cork. I didn't feel like asking them last minute and them having to squeeze me in because they felt sorry for me.

It's so bloody unfair went a hammer in my head and a dull pain started somewhere between my eyebrows. A familiar feeling rose up with the pain:

the feeling that I didn't belong, didn't fit in, didn't have a proper family life and everything around me was rackety and disorganized. Rita and I were like gipsies – chaotic and mad and unsettled, unconventional and arty-farty. *I just hated it.*

All I'd ever wanted was to be ordinary like everyone else, with nice normal aunts and uncles and grandparents, not to mention a brother or sister.

When Rita had been late for the school half-term play (I was the heroine) I'd screamed, "Why can't you be a normal mother?"

She'd snapped back, "And wear Laura Ashley and bake cakes for tea?"

I looked at her now with deep dislike. Her face wore a pained and, yes, I'm glad to say, guilty expression. Good, I thought smugly, feeling gorgeously self-righteous. Serve you right, you ... selfish ... cow!

"Any ideas?" she asked softly.

Usually I prefer to work out things for myself but I wasn't going to waste energy helping her feel better. My face started to cave into a mammoth sulk, which makes me look like Frankenstein. I've given up on being smart, witty and blasé, which come so effortlessly to Grania; or serious and thoughtful like Elizabeth. Maybe that's the real me: mean, tough, cynical. I lowered my eyebrows at Rita to look even fiercer.

Sometimes I'm quite comfortable with this idea of being hard and mean, especially when I've remembered not to brush my thick bushy hair (inherited from my Mauritian father). It's also fun to lay it on a bit. Sometimes I do my shirt buttons out of sync, wear odd socks. It adds to the eccentric image and I find I've become the person I've invented.

"Hmmm?" Rita looked hopefully at me.

In answer I snarled, "I'm not staying with Piloo, that's for sure. I've had enough of her guru."

Piloo's idea of fun was to trail me around Brixton market sifting through second-hand stalls. Her idea of meals was veggie burgers, soya mince, nut rolls, slimy spinach, brown rice. Uggghhh! Her idea of entertainment was to take me to ethnic folk dances at the community centre. Thanks, but no thanks.

"You can't do that anyway. You've forgotten she's off to see her guru, her wonderful guru of Oz." Our eyes met and we started to laugh hysterically; it saved me from throwing something at her.

We stopped when I got the hiccups. *Hic-hic-hic* was the only sound in the kitchen.

"Oh God! Why did this have to happen?" She buried her face in her hands. She reached for the teapot and lit up. *Kill yourself*, I thought. *I don't care any more.*

The skies opened and down it tipped like it had

been waiting for this very moment in my life. With every gust of wind belting rain against the rattling sash window, I had the urge to do something dramatic, to make a statement, to run away from Rita, from Desmond, Piloo, everybody. I wanted to fling myself into the storm outside to see what could happen; to find something new and different.

It came like the claps of thunder tearing the sky apart.

India!

Of course, that's where I'd go – to my grandparents, Nana and Nani.

I remembered their house, on a hillside. The last time I went I was eight: sedate walks holding my grandfather's hand, inspecting the vegetable patch, picking up snails under cabbage leaves, looking across to the next valley; tea with Nani on the verandah, a dainty linen napkin on my lap, eating home-made chewy meringues; being looked after by Hira and Lila who worked for my grandparents and who showed me how to make chapattis.

A huge relief suddenly lightened my mood. Great! That's where I would go! I patted Rita on her knee. "It's all right, Ma. I'll go and stay with Nana and Nani."

She looked doubtful. "What? There's nothing to do in Daroga. You'll be bored rigid in five minutes.

All they do is play golf and bridge. No, no, we'll think of something else."

I simply don't understand this woman. She's got a perfectly nice family, but she acts as though she's an orphan. Which means I don't have functioning grandparents either. They're always writing and sending presents, but the last time we were there – more than five years ago – Rita had a stinking row. She has never talked about it. All I remember is everyone shouting and screaming, doors slamming, and leaving Daroga in a taxi all the way to the airport in Delhi. She just clams up whenever I ask her what happened.

You're probably wondering why I couldn't stay with my father. Well, he's as far away as Nana and Nani. My parents got married (too young, Rita says) when they were students at the University of London, but Ma desperately wanted to follow her ambition and my dad went into politics in Mauritius, so they parted when I was three.

I see my dad once a year when he comes to London for a conference, but he's married to my least favourite person in the world (apart from Piloo's guru) and once a year is enough.

"I suppose you could travel out with Piloo," Ma said in a grudging way half an hour later. She obviously hadn't found another solution.

Arrangements for visa, tickets and inoculations all had to be done in a tearing hurry, but Rita has all the right contacts, so it wasn't really a problem. I wondered how Piloo would react, so I sneakily picked up the extension when Rita phoned to ask if I could travel with her. "Are you sure? Have you decided to let it go at last?"

I wondered if she meant the fight Ma had had with her parents. I should have pestered her a little more, I thought. But I was so young, then. I was sure by the end of my holidays this time it would come together and make sense, so I decided to stop worrying.

In the couple of days before we left I was so excited that I went through every single envelope of photos (no albums in our flat) sorting out pics of my grandparents. I lingered over my nani when she young – she was so glam and so was my nana in his army uniform. There were photos of them with Hira and Lila, their cook and maid. I wondered about the girl who posed with them. Ma said she was called Bina and she was Lila and Hiralal's granddaughter. I hadn't met her on that last visit because she'd gone to stay with an aunt and uncle.

"She's practically been adopted by Nana and Nani. She's a funny little thing, but at least you'll have company," Rita told me.

I did have the feeling that she wanted to say something more, maybe something that would throw light on the estrangement between her and her parents, but she never did, and the next thing it was time to leave.

Rita drove Piloo and me to Heathrow. Terminal 3 was like a fairground with silks and satins and turbans and saris and skullcaps and veiled women. Children ran around playing tag and tripping up people in the departure area. Just before we went through security Rita gave me a carrier bag that weighed a ton. It was stuffed with chocolate and paperbacks for my grandparents. "Indian Cadburys is awful," she grimaced.

Rita is so confident that she never hides her feelings, pulling her face in gargoyle expressions even in public. "Darling Poochi, have a lovely time. I'll try and fix it with the office so I can join you before your holiday's over. We'll come home together," she assured me. She gave me a huge hug and turned away before I could see her crying.

I picked up my rucksack and the carrier bag and walked inside with Piloo trailing behind in her long skirt, beads and many scarves.

Two

🌰

BINA

Some of my worst memories are tied up with my birthdays. The year I turned fifteen was the time Sarla came to Stoneleigh to stay with her grandparents, whom I called Koshy Aunty and Uncleji. At the time I knew her only by name. From the preparations that went on, it seemed everyone was preparing for royalty. My goodness what a fuss there was! Yes, I did feel jealous, but what of it?

My grandparents, Hiralal and Lila Chaubey, who work for Aunty and Uncleji, have brought me up to know my place, to be respectful to my elders and people who are older, wiser, richer – anyone from a higher social class. No one could guess how much that irritates me. If I give other people so much respect and importance and kowtow to them what happens to me? Am I a nobody? Why should I put on this big drama of playing humble pie and Goody Two-Shoes? Maybe if I'd been named Guddi (doll), or Pinky, I would have turned out to be someone who sweetly accepted her lot. But Bina is the name of a musical instrument and I have a voice and a tune of my own.

Actually, I had quietly started changing after I turned twelve or thirteen. Nearly every day I wondered, what should I do when I grow up? It became a complete obsession. I didn't want meekly to agree to be a comma on the page, a little nobody orphan: a servant's child, a dependent girl.

Slowly, slowly, as I thought about the options open to me, the more important I began to feel. I started to feel that my life did matter and I would become independent and strong one day. Of course I didn't rush around blabbing out my thoughts to the world, but I could feel myself changing inside.

I have a clear memory of my birthdays. Twelve, thirteen, fourteen and the birthday from hell, when I turned fifteen. As my special day came nearer, the day I was born and the day my life began, I felt a tightening in my throat. It was like something was waiting to jump out – a phantom shut up inside, or maybe just a shout of laughter, a cry of wonder or joy, it was as though I was waiting and waiting for some wonderful surprise.

Finally I was forced to admit that I was waiting for the person closest to me in blood, my mother; and by the time I turned fifteen, I became brave enough and strong enough to understand that she would never come.

But as for my sixteenth, I was invited to my best friend Mary Lobo's place. Mary Lobo is a gentle girl and never asks me personal questions. She never forces me to share my secrets and so I get on very well with her.

The Lobos live in a set of rooms at the Daroga Club, where all the poshies are members, and Mr Stanley Lobo is the head steward of the club. I only ever see him wearing a white monkey jacket and black trousers. He can balance two trays full of glasses and plates on the flat of each hand, looking as cool as the lemonade in the glass jug.

Mary had put out a plate of pastries covered with smooth chocolate icing ordered by her father from the club chef. We settled ourselves on the sofa with cups of tea and cake to watch *The Sound of Music* (for the fourth time – we loved it so much) and Mary's mother, Janice, was also there, her fingers flying in and out of her knitting.

Mary gave me an Oxford Classics copy of *Jane Eyre* and I got a pair of dangly garnet earrings from Koshy Aunty. My grandparents gave me a box of cambric hankies. I have so many boxes of hankies – printed, embroidered, coloured – stored in my dowry box. I think Grandmother forgets from year to year that I have always had the same present from them!

It was such a lovely peaceful birthday, cent per cent different from the year before. That disastrous day started with a newsflash on Doordarshan TV that Rajiv Gandhi had been blown to bits by a suicide bomber. Our prime minister had just reached for the mike to make his speech at a political meeting in southern India, when a young woman, hair in plaits, neat and innocent in salwar kameez, came out of the crowd and – *whoosh!* – they both went up in an explosion of flame and smoke. Arms and legs and blood went flying everywhere like a horror film of Holi. Lots of people were killed. I wish I'd been a doctor, or even a medical student – I could have helped the injured.

My mother used to kill people, like the avenging goddess Kali. Kali is a fierce and angry goddess. Just think, my mother gave me life, but she herself dealt in death! My feelings about her are very confused: burning anger mixed up with longing for the relationship I never had with her.

After that newsflash, my eyes cloudy with tears, I was milking Gulabi, our beautiful red cow. I pressed my head to her side, sniffing and drinking in deep breaths of her comforting smell of grass and milk, while tears dripped down my cheeks.

My grandmother called out, "When you have put the milk in the kitchen come here, I have a present for you." She always sounded flat, as though every feeling had been ironed out of her. She never gave away any emotion. Her face, too, was empty of expression and the light glinting off her glasses was more lively than the light in her own eyes: not like Julie Andrews. I knew Grandmother had been through very hard times, but I couldn't understand why she was so undemonstrative. "Come, come," (with an accompanying pat on the back) was the nearest she got to showing affection or concern. My mother had always been a problem for her, and because I was her daughter, it must have been the reason Grandmother Lila didn't like me.

So there was no point, really, in telling her about Rajiv and the bomb because she wouldn't have said anything to make me feel better. I finished milking Gulabi and put the brass pot, all frothing and bubbling, next to the stove. Later Grandmother would bring it to the boil and skim off the cream to churn into butter.

On my bed in the front room she had laid out a green sari with a matching petticoat and blouse. It was a hideous colour that reminded me of a jungle parrot, or the paint they use on petrol stations – a very low-class shade. The border and *pallu* was a band of silvery tinsel with a single thread of red running through it. Grandmother has no feeling for beauty or colour. It was depressing that she had resigned herself to such a boring life with my bad-tempered grandfather, her only interest being in little domestic jobs at Koshy Aunty's place.

"Come, come, let me tie it for you. You wear saris in such an untidy way."

She got busy wrapping it round me and measuring five pleats, tucking them flat into the waistband of the petticoat. The rest of the material she passed across my chest and left shoulder so it draped and hung in graceful folds. At school all the girls knew how to tie a sari, but all of us were awkward bundled up in six yards of cloth, like sacks of potatoes. Foreign clothes – imported jeans and dresses copied from *Femina* and *Cosmo* – were much more exciting.

"There," she pursed her lips critically, "now you look like you always should – a properly dressed *woman*."

I hated the sound of the word "woman". It made me feel like a freak. It was so final, so much a fact, and yet I didn't even know what a "woman" was supposed to feel like.

Last time she mentioned that I was a "woman" I shrank with cold inside. Maybe it's different abroad, but in this country, *women* are another species; once you come into *that* category you can never again feel free like a young girl. When my periods started Grandmother shot me a funny look, as though I ought to feel guilty.

"Now you will be able to have babies," she said abruptly. "Never let a man touch you from now on." Of course, I took it to heart and when Uncleji (who my grandparents work for, and whom I see every day) patted me fondly on the head or arm like he often did, I reacted like I'd been electrocuted! I am almost a second granddaughter to him, and Koshy Aunty, who noticed, gave me a different kind of funny look.

"Bina *beti*, what has happened? Has Uncle scolded you about your homework?"

When I explained about my periods she threw up her hands and laughed. I was packed into the car and taken to Duli Ram chemist to buy a six-month supply of sanitary napkins. She sat me down and explained about the birds and bees – in a light sort of way. Before that, believe me, I'd had no idea where babies came from! Mary Lobo and I never ever talked about that sort of thing. But even that jokey explanation wasn't enough to comfort me; I felt very uneasy about what men could do to girls if they wanted to: how they could hurt them, force themselves on them and touch their private parts. That's the reason I didn't want to think about being a woman. I was a girl, an innocent schoolgirl, and I would *always* be one.

I was even shy about the fact that I had to wear a bra. Being a woman came in a package with dangerous and embarrassing things: sanitary pads, sweaty armpits, fears of getting pregnant, breasts ... and of course *BOYS*!

Now the reason my fifteenth birthday was the worst birthday of my life is tied up with that horrible sari. You can't run or cycle wearing a sari, you have to behave like a ... *woman*. From frocks I had gone to salwar kameez. Blue and white for school, and any colour I wanted for home, except if I came home late because Bannerji or Merriweather had kept me in for extra work. Then it wasn't worth changing.

Grandmother wagged a finger. "Tomorrow you wear your new sari, exactly like I showed you. We have visitors, so make sure you wash your face, freshen up with Charmis cream and powder. Comb and plait your hair nicely after you get back from school."

I was immediately alert. "Who's coming?" Maybe

my mother! "Tell me who, why won't you tell me?"

Why did Grandmother bustle out pretending she hadn't heard?

Next day, after school, I helped to make spinach pakoras. Who were all these preparations for? On the white tablecloth (embroidered with yellow and red flowers by me) she placed a dish of almond *barfi* and *jalebis* from the market, along with bottles of Fanta and Coke with straws ready. Then I put on the sari. Grandfather was still at Koshy Aunty and Uncleji's, finishing the washing up from lunch, but he would soon be back.

Grandmother gave me one final inspection. She tugged the back hem of my sari to make it fall straight and even, straightened up and pulled impatiently at the gold chain I always wear. "Take this off!" Hanging from the chain is a locket that was my mother's, the only thing I have of hers.

I dusted the front room and plumped the cushions worked by me in cross-stitch. It doubled as my own room, but the bedspread of orange *phulkari* work on the divan disguised it as a sitting area. At her instructions I arranged five straight-backed chairs from other parts of the house along the wall. It looked like a criminal was going to be cross-examined in court.

Grandmother said, go, hurry and pick some marigolds from the temple garden, so I went next door hoping I wouldn't bump into the priest with the sly peeping eyes.

I had just crammed the flowers into a brass vase when Grandfather entered with the visitors, and like the beam of a torch lighting up a dark room, I suddenly saw the reason for the preparations: the marigolds, the dressing up, the powder on my face, the pale pink lipstick that Grandmother had rubbed with a finger on my lower lip.

He sat between his parents, awkward, hardly looking up to answer my grandfather's questions in monosyllables. His whole body drooped and his hair hung in separate, oily strands; his face was bumpy and shiny with pimples. All three of them studied me. I could have been a creature in a zoo. What were his parents thinking as they watched me in my green sari, taking around the *barfi* and *jalebis* and handing out the paper serviettes?

"Sooo, you will finish your tenth year soon?"

"Your grandfather says you are a homely girl. Did you make the pakoras?" Patting the cushion, "Is this your embroidery?" . "Can you knit sweaters? Do you sing, or play the harmonium?"

"Have you been to Ambala?"

After my "job interview", Grandfather and the

boy's father started chatting about their time in the army and the two women talked about nothing much, while the pimply boy and I sat with our eyes fixed on the floor. Funny how many things I'd never before noticed: the cat-shaped ink stain on the carpet; the scuffs on the chairlegs; bits of dust dancing in the afternoon sunbeam.

After they'd left, hot tears spurted from my eyes when Grandfather barked, "Well what do you say? They want an engagement as soon as possible. He has excellent qualifications – a degree in refrigeration engineering from Roorkee, a scooter and no worries. He's an only son so they all live together in a big bungalow and Ambala is a nice cantonment town. His father and I were in the army. He was General Dewan's orderly and retired on full pension after being awarded two medals."

I shouted at him, something I had never dared to do before. "Is that all I'm worth? A pimply youth with a scooter?"

My hysterics didn't seem to bother Grandfather. He walked away dismissively.

"You know my views and they will never be any different. Girls need to settle early and start a family. They should never have to work outside the home. Luckily, this boy can look after you and you will fit in well with the joint family."

Settle, settle, settle. Mud settled at the bottom of a river. My river went on raging like a mountain torrent. I barely controlled myself that day.

Grandfather's sergeant-major voice, the bullying tone, was all I ever heard. Who was he to decide the map of my life? Oh, Hiralal Chaubey was a difficult man, storming off, shouting, then not speaking for days to Grandmother or me; moody, narrow-minded, conservative, suspicious, sometimes even quite scary. But knowing all this, I wasn't prepared for the enormous show of power and authority. I couldn't believe how trapped and helpless it made me feel.

When I turned to Grandmother, her lips were set in a straight line as usual. There would be no support from her.

That same evening we watched the news on TV. A day later the same story was still playing over and over again. First Rajiv's fair, mild, round face, his Italian wife Sonia with the long brown ironed hair we so admired at school, their children Rahul and Priyanka; then explosions, shouting, people running, confusion and the later shots of Sonia crying at home and the small children looking sad. The dam that kept in all my sorrow and despair crashed and I started to sob wildly; though if it was for Rajiv or just myself, I couldn't tell you.

Next day I dawdled back from school, snapping

twigs and leaves from the roadside hedge and crushing them in my fingers. What was I going to do if I couldn't carry my plans forward? The dreams I had hugged close to me since I was twelve, of becoming a doctor and leaving Daroga to live my own life ... of being lifted on a magic carpet to somewhere far away – Delhi, or even Bombay. My dreams had kept me going. What if they never came true?

I stopped at Stoneleigh, Uncleji and Koshy Aunty's house, for tea and sandwiches and to do my homework under their kindly supervision. The expression on my face made Auntyji ask what had happened, so I related the events of the afternoon before: the tea party, the sari, and Pimply from Ambala.

She sighed heavily. "Can't you get it into that old dinosaur," and she rapped her manicured nails on the table, "that he must stop trying to play God? There will be plenty of time to think about a marriage after Bina gets her qualifications. She has enough on her plate cramming for these wretched exams and keeping up with the other girls."

Uncleji sighed even louder, threw down the book he was reading, and called out, "Hiralal! Are you in the kitchen? Please could you finish what you're doing and come here right away. I need to discuss something."

Auntyji and I retreated to another room while the two men talked. They had known each other like brothers for something like forty years and neither minced his words. Grandfather Hiralal had been working as Uncleji's batman since he joined the army as a smart young lieutenant, until the day he retired as a three-star general.

Koshy Aunty, always careful never to criticize my grandparents to my face, said soothingly, "You know Hira – he just wants to remind the world that he is in charge of his family, that he is Mr Boss. Typical male! He knows full well we'll never allow you to be married off at such a young age."

"At no age," I sulked. "I *will* go to Chandigarh, to Government Medical College, and study to be a doctor. They think they can fix my fate just like that. I'll show them!" To my shame I started to wail like a baby. "After what happened to my mother?" I knelt and clutched Auntyji's knees desperately, like a beggar in the bazaar. "Don't let them do that to me!"

"I won't, Bina. Don't worry, *bittia*, I promise not to let anything bad happen to you." She smoothed my back with long fingers. It was rigid as a wooden board on which you roll chapattis. What would happen if she and Uncleji weren't there to protect me?

Oh, how I was hungry for hugs; hungry for people to like me, to love me and be interested in me.

Not ever, even in my dreams, would I have thrown myself into Grandmother or Grandfather's arms. It never occurred to me that I should ever reveal anything intimate or important about myself to them. Though we lived under the same roof and shared the same family name. I tried really hard to be good and behave like they had taught me; to think about family honour, or *izzat*, duty, obedience, modesty (keeping my eyes on the ground when I went to the bazaar or school). But my heart, my feeling side, where I felt safe about showing anger, sadness, wonder, cutting jokes, complaining about school – all that I kept to share with Koshy Aunty and Uncleji. They had been my second grandparents since I was little and they knew me better than my own blood relatives. They loved the side of me that I like, the side that's free to be playful and silly like a small child, without any worries.

I knew that Koshy Aunty, especially, liked to listen to me. But they are both so wonderful! They care about every small-small thing. Auntyji notices when I am out of kirby grips or hair clips; if I need a new pair of sandals, a pen or a school book. They would really have liked me to stay with them all the time, but it would have upset my grandparents (family honour) and shown them up as being incompetent.

So Uncleji had agreed on a compromise. They would choose which school I attended, look after my fees at the Convent of the Immaculate Conception and pay for my dance lessons with Antonia. My teacher Antonia is a brilliant Bharata Natyam dancer. She is English, but has chosen to live with her cats and dogs in Daroga.

So it's easy to understand why I spend most of my time in Stoneleigh, being helped with schoolwork, reading the newspapers, practising my English. Uncleji is strict about my studies. He pushes me all the time: work hard, top your exams and go to college. But Auntyji and he are very careful to keep Grandfather sweet. Nothing will change him being so traditional and *ziddi* – so stubborn and fixed in his ideas. It takes the tact of a saint to get along with him.

Auntyji's friends are always complaining about their "Nep" servants. Nepalis have this bad reputation for robbing and murdering their employers. Everyone says it's because they can catch a train to Nepal and hide out in their mountain villages where they can't be traced. It's hard for me to face it, but Auntyji and Uncleji are growing old. In winter he gets bronchitis and she suffers from arthritis. Their two daughters, Rita and Piloo, live far away in

England and they rely on my grandparents to take care of their parents and run the house; so Koshy Aunty and Uncleji can't afford to rock the boat with Grandfather, or they would end up at the mercy of "Nep" cooks and maids.

How to describe such a complicated life? I get dizzy when I try to see myself for who I really am: my mother's daughter; Koshy Aunty's "adopted" grandchild; the only granddaughter of Hira and Lila, the cook and maid; an innocent schoolgirl swotting hard for exams; or a "grown woman" being presented for marriage. There are so many Binas in one person. Maybe I feel like this because it's not *my* life, but one that belongs to the people who run it for me. I'm like a doll that jerks up and down in the hands of a puppeteer at a village fair.

Plus, there are all my secrets, which I'm not allowed to share with anyone, not even Mary. Mary says, give your life to Jesus and He will show you the way and make you into a new person. Once she gave me such a pretty card with a softly smiling Our Lady dressed in a blue robe – like a pink and white version of Mary Lobo herself – and a prayer printed in gold lettering. She has worked out her future and is planning to join Mother Theresa's nuns after she finishes college. Everything will be taken care of by Jesus, she says. But me, I don't want someone else to work out my future, and I don't believe in any kismet-shismet. I have to find my own destiny, or else there is no future for me. If I don't, then it will end up being the future that's been planned by my grandfather, and I would rather die than go along with that!

I am so different from the other girls at school. I can't hide the fact that my grandparents work for Koshy Aunty and Uncleji, who pay my school fees. Just that sets me apart! Of course Mary's father is a steward at the club, but he isn't a domestic servant. And though the Hindu majority at school look down on Christians and call them "converts", "mission kids" or "chee-chees", I am even lower than the Christian girls: you see, *I am servant class*.

Funny when you think the creamy layer need their servants to cook and clean, wash and polish and mend for them, but their servants aren't *persons* for them. They only exist to serve their masters, like donkeys.

So it's hardly surprising that I don't belong to any gang at school. Mary has her Catholic group and disappears with Yvonne, Delphine, Philomena and Dorothy to mass and retreats and catechism; in her quiet way, Mary has managed to slip into her place at our posh school. She knows exactly who she is – she's secure in her identity. Mother Imelda

Rosario is like a protective hen to her Catholic girls – she does her best not to let them be bullied or made to feel small.

But me, I'm the servant's child and almost invisible. Sometimes I catch Madhu or Sumita deliberately wrinkling their noses when I come near. I don't smell, so it could only mean that they want me to know *they* know I come from what in their eyes is the gutter.

Just imagine what these snobbish girls would do if they knew who I really am; if they knew the secret of my mother! Carrying this secret around is such a heavy load that sometimes I can hardly lift my eyes, or my feet or even laugh out loud. I can't be noticed. If someone finds out my secret I'll have to leave school straightaway. There will be such a hue and cry that Sister Imelda won't have any choice but to ask me to go. Parents will be so scandalized that they will pull their precious daughters out of school in case I contaminate them, like an infectious disease!

Then, if I do leave, all doors will shut with a loud bang. The prison will grow real walls. Grandfather will arrange a marriage *phataphat*, double-quick, and nobody will be able to stop them sending me to Ambala or some other horrible little town. *Get rid of her before the news gets around!*

Sometimes I weep for my mother. There are moments I wish we were together, like a normal mother and daughter. But then I become so angry that I beat my pillow. Look what she did – run away and abandon me! Abandon me to be pushed about here and there! Abandon me to my grandfather's ideas of who I ought to be, what I should do, whom I should marry!

Then I quickly glance at her photo, a black and white one, all creased and faded, and see the face of a stranger.

When I last met her, ten years back, I was just six years old. Grandmother dressed me up in my favourite pink dress with a satin flounce and the red Bata sandals, so big that my feet swam in them. She oiled and combed my hair into a "fountain" style with a rubber band and the three of us went by train to a place down in the plains, far from our hill station.

It was the middle of summer and the temperature must have been in the hundreds. I remember my eyes closing with the heat and glare, and I was so drowsy that I fell asleep. I wasn't used to the heat, living in Daroga, more than 1500 metres above sea level. My grandparents and I took a *tonga* from the station and it clip-clopped to the jail where we were escorted through huge, tall wooden gates. The walls inside were dazzling white, very high, and all the windows in the buildings had bars.

I remember a hot, bright compound with a neem tree. There was no breeze, but we waited in its deep shade. I remember a squirrel running down the trunk and running up again. It disappeared into the leafy branches. Then I saw a woman they called my mother walking towards us. She didn't hurry. Actually, I remember she stopped quite far away to look, her hand shading her eyes against the glare of the sun. One step at a time she advanced, uncertainly, fearfully like she was walking on hot coals. She wore a grey prison sari and I saw her sad eyes and her hair showing white in the parting. She called in a strange, high-pitched voice, "Come, come here, *gudiya*, my little doll," and moved nearer to touch my face. She pulled me close to her, till I felt I couldn't breathe, so I wriggled away. I didn't like her musty body smell and felt suffocated. I glared at her, angry and unsettled. She sat back on her heels and cried aloud, "My own child hates me! *Hai Ishwar*, may I die!"

I ran and hid behind my grandmother. I was so frightened by this strange woman with desperation coming from the pit of her stomach, from the lap in which she'd tried to hold me, and I couldn't feel anything, never mind love, for her – this person they said was my mother.

Grandmother made a feeble attempt to push me towards her. "We don't behave like this," she scolded; but what had I done? It was all the strange woman's fault!

"Oh, what is the use of anything, now we are all disgraced," grandfather said bitterly. He made no move to touch his daughter, or to offer any comfort.

My mother is called Shobharani, which means queen of beauty. But she wasn't beautiful then. She had wild, staring eyes, her hair was all tangled and her breath was stale. She started to cry noisily, beating her breasts and then her forehead. She wailed and sobbed, all hunched up, squatting on her heels, and I remember my heart turned over.

The warden came running and slapped her hard and I screamed, "Don't hit her, don't hit my mother!"

They led her away roughly by the shoulder. My grandfather picked me up in his arms. Suddenly I was high off the ground, safe once more. We turned our backs on her and the warden lady.

We returned to Daroga in silence. I haven't seen her since.

Three

BINA

It's July and the new school year begins in two weeks, then, soon after that, we'll have mock exams. So here I am at my desk, in the glazed verandah at Stoneleigh, forcing myself to cram history dates. First War of Independence: 1857. Rani of Jhansi, who fought on horseback against the British: 1858. Indian National Congress: 1888... Oh, I really hate history – all those dead people and things that went on long ago. What possible difference can they make? I am much more interested in *now* and what's going to happen in the future.

Today the sky is a clear blue. The monsoon hasn't started. The hillside is green with pine trees; I see orange butterflies flitting over the canna lilies. It's a beautiful afternoon. I suppose I am lucky to be in my position – so much better off than a girl from a village, or a girl who goes to the local government school. I wish I could *feel* in my heart that I am a lucky person, instead I'm always anxious and worried, always thinking something bad is going to happen.

My grandparents have gone for their afternoon rest to their own little house, which is in the hamlet behind Stoneleigh. Koshy Aunty and Uncleji are playing golf at the club. Carmen, the faithful black and white dog, is sitting on my feet keeping them warm. I can hear Bholuram the gardener singing in his cracked fluty voice. Could it be the song the villagers sing about my mother in the hills all around Daroga?

Goddess Shobharani rey
You are queen of all the hills
Devi Shobharani rey
Let the mountains sing your praises.

The crow must be your brother now
The kite your brother's wife
Their nests will be your hiding place
Their perch shall guard your life.

Devi Shobharani rey
You are queen of all the hills
Goddess Shobharani rey
The mountains shout your praises.

I love the tune, it is like a melancholy memory; if you listen to the wind in the pines, the hills throw back the song it makes, and my biro has written down the words as though someone was writing for me. Automatic writing, like when you put a little talcum powder on the table to let the glass slide, and place your fingers lightly on its upturned base. Does he love me, does he not love me, does he even know I exist? I carry on writing and this time the words say: My dearest Mother, how are you? When will I see you again?

I laugh, wondering, why am I doing this? It's a useless exercise, since I don't even know if she reads the letters I have sent her.

How I long for her love! The love I've never known, but only imagined. How I long for her arms round me, to put my head on her lap.

They tell me blood is thicker than water, but to me these are empty words. I feel a kind of closeness with her, but the reality is that it doesn't exist. Doesn't *my* existence mean anything to her?

When they come back from golf, Uncleji will test me on dates, so I should keep going. I'm really not bad at maths and science, but forget about arts subjects – so boring! English just gives me a headache and Bannerji is always saying, Bina how will you ever make it? I borrow Denzil's (that's Mary Lobo's brother) notes and essays and crib from them, otherwise Shakespeare and Wordsworth would be complete double Dutch!

Oof, nothing sticks in my head today; all those facts are disappearing like mist in the sun. That's what the villagers say about my mother; that she used to come in the night and vanish like mountain mist at dawn. *Come on Bina, buck up and concentrate!*

For the ten plus two exams I have to aim for high marks – more than eighty-five per cent if I want admission to medical college. The competition for places is tough. Everyone knows doctors make a lot of money, but that's not *my* reason for studying medicine. Girls and boys from rich, well-connected families pull strings to get in, but I must compete with brainpower alone. So much to study, so much to remember. The best strategy is to keep focused on my dream to leave Daroga and go somewhere far away.

When I was younger my mother meant nothing to me, but now I miss her.

I miss more the idea of a mother than anything else: a mother who is all mine, who will take care of me, take my side, be there always. I have a drawer full of exercise books with imaginary letters that I have written and not sent. She is the mother of my imagination, of my dreams, so I can believe anything I want.

The villagers tell many stories about her bravery. In caves all over the hills there are little shrines to her where they go on pilgrimage and pray for their sick, both animals and human. They think of her as a goddess, which makes me proud. At the same time I am ashamed, since it's only villagers who believe she is a great person. The rest of the world thinks she is a great criminal. The villagers are waiting for her to come back and they believe this with religious faith. One day I think it's all true – that she is a heroine; the next day I know she is a poor, crazy woman who has completely forgotten she gave birth to me, her daughter, a girl like herself.

I am forbidden ever to talk about her, or even mention her name, but Antonia, my dance teacher, secretly tells me stories about her. From her I found out that my mother was fourteen years old when my grandmother, Lila, married her off. Fourteen – two whole years younger than me!

Grandfather Hira had gone off to fight some war against the Chinese near the Tibetan border and when he didn't come back with the other soldiers they thought he must be dead, but he had been taken prisoner. Grandmother Lila fell into a terrible depression and became very ill, so when someone from our village came to her with an offer of marriage for my mother, Grandmother was only too glad to take the easy way out. She handed over Shobharani to another family because she couldn't face the responsibility of looking after a beautiful young girl by herself. Shobha was starting to be eyed by the men in the bazaar, and everyone knew her father wasn't there to protect her. Grandmother was scared that her teenage daughter would be molested and gossiped about, or even raped, which happens all the time in our part of the world.

Now it's easy to understand why I panic and think they will pack me off, just like they did with my mother. In these parts no one has any use for girls. Daughters don't create wealth – they are only useful for producing babies: boy babies, that is. A daughter is a curse. She can be fair game for any man, she can ruin the family name, and then no one will marry her. She needs a lot spent on her marriage and dowry, or she won't get a husband. *She is inferior.* This kind of thinking has a terrible effect on girls, it makes us ashamed: ashamed of our gender, ashamed of our body, ashamed to wear nice things. It doesn't occur to people that girls also have brains; that they can get good jobs like boys. If they are educated they can stand on their own feet, earn, drive cars and scooters, be independent and look after their parents. It never occurs to anyone that they might not want to get married, for God's sake!

Look at what happened to Shobharani.

After she was married off, she got pregnant every single year, and every time the baby died. Her mother-in-law said she was a witch and began cursing her. She cursed her for not bringing enough dowry: her gold bangles, silk saris, cooking pots and pans weren't enough for the old woman. She wanted bags of cash, a fridge, scooter, electric fans. She took pleasure in making Shobha work for the whole family like a menial – cooking, cleaning, washing everyone's clothes by hand, scrubbing. She was slapped and pinched and her ears were twisted and no one ever stopped her husband – my so-called father – from beating Shobha black and blue.

Every time she ran away to Hira and Lila, they hauled her back to her useless husband and cruel in-laws. That's the way it is with lots of families – it's the fear of disgrace, you see.

Then I was born and I survived, but I was a girl … and it was all Shobha's fault. She wasn't talented enough to bear a son! So my father would drink country liquor and thump my mother, just for the hell of it. She bore this treatment for seventeen years! Either his chapattis were too hot or cold, or too thick or too thin. Or she had no cash handy, or there didn't have to be any reason. Shobha told Antonia how his face would swell with hatred and rage, and how he would throw curses at her like kitchen slops. It went on and on until she might well have died. But one day he went too far. She was squatting on the floor rolling out chapattis. She got up from her haunches and hit him with the rolling pin and…

They locked her up without food or water for a week. I was only little and I cried without stopping. At least it put my father in a wheelchair, but Shobha ran away for good, leaving me behind.

I was two.

She never even answers Antonia's letters. She can't concentrate on anything, because she is quite mental after all her experiences. She doesn't remember that once upon a time she had a daughter.

Blood is thicker than water? Don't make me laugh!

Maybe this is the time to mention another complication. I feel shy talking about this, because well brought up girls are not supposed to spend time thinking about boys; but there are these two fellows. The one I like a lot is called Sidhartha. He's eighteen and a fresher at Chandigarh University, where he is studying to be a doctor. He will qualify in six years. He is so handsome and out of my league really because he is from one of the grandest families in the state. His aunt, Princess Vidyakumari of

Daroga, has been a lifelong friend of Koshy Aunty and Uncleji. She plays golf with them and she's a little crazy and eccentric. How mad she'll be if she finds out that her nephew is my secret hero! Of course, nothing has happened between us (how could it? He doesn't even know my name!) but the princess is very snobbish and self-conscious about her ancestors. Her royal blood makes her top shelf, even higher than the other "hi-fis"!

The second fellow is someone I hate. His name is Jeevan and he works for Uncleji as a driver. He lurks around, thinking he's very smart. He likes tight drainpipes and polyester shirts; he has a pencil moustache and long hair and models himself on a Bollywood star – always humming some *filmi geet* and leering. What we call a slimy "eve-teaser".

I could ignore him, but I see him every day. The worst is that he's obsessed about marrying me. He thinks he has some kind of God-given right because he comes from the same caste and class as me. The terrible thing is that last week he said he knew the secret of my mother! He said if I didn't marry him he would tell everyone in Daroga that I was her daughter.

Because my mother ran away from her married home – which is many miles away – no one guessed that she was Hira and Lila's daughter. When she was jailed, she always refused to say anything about her background and family. Her in-laws would be too ashamed to claim her, so her identity remained unknown. If people in Daroga get to hear that Shobharani is my mother, and a jailbird no less, it will be *tata* to my plans for higher studies. The parents of the girls at school will insist that I am expelled, and I will become an outcaste like her.

I am frightened. I don't know what to do. If I tell Jeevan to jump into a well, he'll spread stories about me and if I complain about him my grandfather will say it's all my fault for leading him on. (I'm a girl, remember, and girls are always in the wrong.) Grandfather's trump card is Pimply from Ambala. Then Aunty and Uncleji will be powerless to stop him.

It is all so complicated:

After my exams are finished, we get a short break. I can't wait, because Antonia is taking me trekking in the hills to meet a man who is a genius at painting pictures. Yesterday at my lesson, she jangled her ankle bells and pirouetted, waving a blue airmail letter. "Guess what? Piloo's coming with us!" Piloo is Purnima, Koshy Aunty's older daughter. She lives in London, England, and comes to India once a year to see her parents and visit her guru in Bangalore. She and Antonia are best friends.

Then another surprise happened this afternoon, just as I started on my trigonometry homework. Koshy Aunty came and stood by my desk. She seemed strangely happy, almost in another world. She was smiling dreamily.

"Bina, I have heard the best news ever! Sarla is coming to spend her holidays with us. She's travelling with Piloo, and Uncleji will fetch them both from New Delhi airport. Her mother is being sent to some far-off country on work, so Sarla is spending the summer here. I just got a call from Rita. It's going to be simply wonderful. We haven't seen our granddaughter for five years!"

Rita and Piloo are sisters. Rita is divorced and Sarla must be fourteen. It's funny how we've never met. Maybe I won't like her, maybe I will. All I know is that when she and Rita came six years ago there was a big fight with Uncleji and Aunty. My grandfather says that's the reason why they've never been back. He sometimes gets a letter from Rita, but her own parents never do. I wonder why that is?

In front of Sarla I have to keep up the story of my parents being killed in a road accident. My grandfather said in his horrible bullying voice, "Your mother's name must never be mentioned. Understand?" I think he hates his own daughter.

"You do understand, don't you, *beti*?" Koshy Aunty told me in her kindly way. "It will be too confusing for the child. Maybe later, when you know each other … for now, the less you talk about your own family the better. Sarla doesn't know India and doesn't understand our ways. Let's go gently."

Four

Four

❧

SARLA

Deep down I'm not all that cynical, or hard or mean – more soft-centred and especially vulnerable (or gullible, if you like) to first impressions; so I was a bit overwhelmed when I stepped into that Air India plane and was immediately transported to another planet. Sitar music twanging, hostesses with the super-cool haughtiness of sari-clad princesses. I watched in awe as they stretched up to stow hand luggage in lockers, showing acres of midriff, then bent down to arrange cots, bestow drinks and shimmy up and down the aisles, treating anxious passengers to a superior lift of their eyebrows.

A whiff of curry escaped from the galley as I hunted for my seat – the princesses were in no mood to help me find it, they were too busy flirting with the male flight attendants. I was sitting miles away from Piloo. Every seat was taken, wall to wall with whole families: mummies and daddies, kiddies and uncles and aunties, grannies and grandpas travelling to meet up with their relatives. I had been curious about how Indian families were with one another, and here I had a ringside seat. "Family" had always been something other people did and which I wanted more than anything for myself. That belonging, being inside a magic circle, was incredibly glamorous and exciting and soon I'd know what it really felt like! I was on my way to be with my own family, to spend my holidays with "my own blood", which sounds so corny but was such a thrilling prospect for me.

I found my window seat and made myself a little nest with pillows and blanket, took out a tube of Fruit Gums, opened the first page of *Rebecca* and settled down happily. Then I felt my neighbour's elbow taking over my arm rest, so I pushed back ever so slightly just to show what was what. No effect. The old lady drew up her knees, resting her bare heels on the seat and I heard her pop a fart. I still haven't worked out the etiquette of farting in front of strangers: say "excuse me", look breezily unconcerned, or place the blame on someone else by making subtly outraged faces like raising your eyebrows and blinking rapidly. No "pardon" was forthcoming from my neighbour, so I turned sideways to give her a proper look-over. She wore salwar kameez with a lacy white dupatta sitting lightly on her head. It kept slipping and she busied herself adjusting it with a great jangling of gold bangles that rode up her forearms. She let out more wind – this time a gusty sigh – and gave me a sweet smile.

Her husband had a long white beard and an enormous turban tied like a jaunty flying saucer. When I got used to seeing lots of Sikhs in India, I noticed how many different turban-tying styles there are: head-hugging and bullet-shaped, pleated and pointed, Frisbee-shaped, white and black, pink, mauve, green, plain colours, prints and stripes. Maybe they come off the peg, or maybe they're tied a different way each morning. It must be very hot with all that cloth wrapped round your long hair.

Anyway, the old Sikh also gave me a nice smile and held out a whole block of Fruit and Nut broken into squares. "Have, *beta*, have," he urged in a croaky old man's voice. Later I found out that *beta* means "my child". His missis pressed my arm in a kindly way, so I couldn't go on being peevish about the trespassing and farting any more. I smiled back, thanked him and offered my Fruit Gums, but they both refused, tapping their dentures.

By now the old lady had oozed fully into my

space. She pulled up her blanket, thoroughly at home on the plane. Soon after take-off, one of the princesses dumped a meal of chicken curry on the little fold-down table and I dived into it because I was starving. After that, even *Rebecca* was too feeble to hold my attention, and for most of the ten-hour journey I snoozed, which is that lovely halfway state between daydreaming and drowsing. Everyone else was sleeping like babies, mouths open and snoring: gently, aggressively or with little whistling noises.

In my favourite dream, I had been adopted by Grania's parents. They, her three brothers and sister are brilliant and I simply adore them.

I could picture them in Cork with all the cousins, aunts, uncles and grandparents. I'd been invited twice, and they were the best times of my life. There were so many of us in that big rambling country house that it began humming with activity early in the morning: doors opening and closing, footsteps, voices (starting low, progressively becoming louder through the day), smells of coffee and cooking.

I don't think Grania and I ever slept in after eight in the morning. We would run through the wet grass in bare feet and plunge into the little river at the bottom of the garden. After a few strokes and lots of splashing we'd run back to the kitchen, tingling and fresh. Mushrooms on toast and eggs and bacon never tasted so good. I could have eaten three platefuls! After stuffing ourselves we'd make sandwiches and go off on bikes for the day. I could imagine what I was missing this summer – charades, sardines, murder in the dark, trips to the fleapit in town, exploring downstream, fishing from the dinghy, car treasure hunts, cards by the fire and everyone so jolly and good-humoured.

Even fights, tears and sulks were bearable because they happened out in the open, usually in front of other people. Not like our sour little squabbles at home where only the furniture was witness to my spite and Ma's sarcasm. In Grania's clan someone or other would step in and restore normality. It was like being snuggled inside a lovely warm duvet, safe and comfortable.

Grania, her cousin – who was fifteen and had curly red hair – and I were always plotting to get away from the younger ones, who had their own cunning ways of tracking and tormenting us with their presence. Oh, what was Sam like this year? Would I still think he was the most attractive boy in the world?

It was time to switch to another delicious daydream – this one about Elizabeth, so incredibly square and self-possessed, with her Alice bands, and home-knitted woollies and walking holidays.

So proper, but she has this genius for saying just the right thing to calm me down, or cheer me up. Just knowing she's chosen me for a special friend makes me feel good inside. Her family are like her, reassuringly orderly and traditional with routines, rituals, mapped out and well-trodden.

For example, Elizabeth and her granny go to Saturday evening mass and once a month they trot down to Selfridges, then lunch in the same Italian cafe that her granny's been going to for twenty-four years! Almost all her clothes are made by her Aunt Jill, which of course I wouldn't be seen dead in (Liberty print blouses with Peter Pan collars, dirndl or A-line skirts) but they choose the material and patterns together. I am so envious. She has a nice older brother and you can actually see that they're fond of one another. She's so lucky.

"Look, there he is, there's Papa!" Piloo's tactful whispery voice rose to a girlish cry, her face red with excitement and the heat that must have been edging up to thirty-eight degrees. My head was compressed into a block of cement, my T-shirt stuck to my back, my teeth felt mossy to my tongue and it was hard to breathe normally. The air had a strange soupy, musty smell. I searched the crowds for Nana until at last I spotted a white-haired, stick-like figure with a bristly moustache in a lined face, waving slowly. There was a lot of pushing and shoving and I suddenly felt horribly out of place. Couldn't I just turn round and go back with the plane that had brought me to Delhi? But what to? The dusty Bayswater flat? To Rita, somewhere miles from civilization? To Grania and Elizabeth, enjoying themselves, and quite oblivious to my loneliness?

"Dear little Sarla," my grandfather welcomed me with the lightest of hugs, like a breath or sigh. For the moment that he held my face his hands felt like dry leaves. "Not so little now!" He stepped back, a hand on my shoulder. "Your Nani's been baking cakes and making meringues and goodness knows what all week. Now. A little breakfast before we set off? There's a long, seven hour journey ahead." He was trying out how to talk to me – not too babyish, not too grown-up either, trying to give me confidence that he was there to protect me. He hadn't had much practice being a grandfather to me.

"Piloo, my dear. Your flight. Not for another three hours. Let's eat something with us now?"

This must be how old soldiers speak, I thought; sort of clipped and jerky and used to giving orders. But the ends of his sentences trailed off uncertainly. And then someone else would be left to pick up the thread and continue the conversation. He was a bit *wispy* like Piloo.

Why were we hanging around the porch with my suitcase and hand luggage when we'd have been cooler inside the terminal building? Out of the milling crowd of people an extremely thin young man came and picked up my suitcase and the carrier bag. He had an old-fashioned pencil moustache and was wearing white trousers and shirt. He kept his eyes on the ground, but I felt he was looking at me. He was a bit creepy looking.

"Jeevan, our driver," Nana explained. "Getting so old now, I can't see too well on the roads." He addressed Jeevan, "We'll be another hour or so. Found some shade for the car? Get a cup of tea and an omelette while we have breakfast."

"Wait," Piloo retrieved the carrier from Jeevan. "These chocolates will melt. Rita sent these for you and Mummy."

"Oh." Wasn't that a funny response? Nana didn't ask any questions about my mother. He hadn't seen her for six years! You'd think he'd want to ask a few questions at least. I suddenly felt a bit sad. This wasn't how families were supposed to behave. What could have gone wrong between father and daughter?

I looked at Piloo to see her reaction, but she

was probably practising her meditation, because she looked far away. I pictured Rita in army fatigues, crouching behind sandbags and I crossed my fingers. *Promise me you won't get killed*, I shot her a telepathic message.

The air-conditioning had broken down and ceiling fans swirled hot, musty air from one end of the restaurant to the other. Nana ordered tea and toast and omelettes. There were burgers and chips on the grease-marked menu, but Nana wouldn't let me have them. He and Piloo chatted away while I slumped in a semi-conscious state from jet lag, staring at three fat businessmen smacking their lips and burping through mountains of food. They discussed deals with podgy hands, fingers stuffed into diamond rings, and shrewd eyes which took in more than they gave out. Their mobile phones kept ringing, but they weren't in a hurry; they seemed to have all the time in the world as they lazily took their calls and chortled with laughter, feeling their layers of chins with their fingers.

One of them caught me staring and gave me a knowing wink, so I shifted my attention to another table where a bride and groom sat in glum silence waiting for their honeymoon flight, while their relatives laughed and teased them. I knew she was a bride because she was wearing a red sari and was dripping with gold jewellery, which must have been suffocating her. I wondered why they looked as though they had nothing to do with one another – perhaps they hardly knew each other, perhaps it was an arranged marriage.

Something grazed my foot. Thinking it was a rat I nearly screamed and kicked out, but then I saw it was a man swabbing the floor with a cloth. Squatting on his haunches, he moved in crab-like motions, making damp half circles on the marble floor. I'd forgotten about people like him who worked in jobs where no one paid much attention to them: they were a bit like human vacuum cleaners and washing machines. The disinfectant on the floor wafted up a strong smell of public toilet. I drew up my knees, starting to feel sick and wishing we could leave. My brain wasn't working at its usual rate. I looked at the wedding party. I was the only outsider. I wasn't part of this world. It had nothing to do with me and I wasn't in control of anything.

Piloo was droning on about her social work and Nana was nodding as he listened to her. You could tell they were father and daughter, with their same pale North Indian skin and beaky nose. My mother has smooth brown skin and her nose is small and snub like mine.

"You could do all that and more here. So many

needs, so much poverty..." Nana was murmuring when I felt faint and knew I was going to be sick. I threw up spectacularly, all over the floor.

"It's the heat ... the excitement ... she's very worried about Rita in the war zone ... hope she'll be all right with you and Mummy..." Piloo cradled me in her bony arms and dabbed my forehead with a wet hanky. I wanted to tell her to get off and buzz off to her fuzzy guru, her fuzzbuzz, her Rolex wizard, but then I noticed her eyes, magnified behind their owlish glasses, looking really worried. I took comfort in her concern.

"Will you manage all right, Sally?" she whispered. She called me that sometimes when she was trying to be affectionate. "Promise you'll phone me in Bangalore if you want me to come to Daroga? You know I'll come straightaway if you're miserable, don't you? Anyway, I'll see you at the end of the holidays. Don't forget to go and see my friend Antonia. She's lovely."

I found myself nuzzling her shoulder like a lost puppy (difficult with her sharp bones) feeling grateful, never having thought before that she really cared about me or had the talent to guess what was going on behind my cool front.

"I'll be OK, don't worry," I managed to say.

The cleaner had cleaned up the horrible mess.

Nana gave him some money for his trouble. "Thank you, sahib," he said, bobbing his head and giving me a shy smile.

The waiter brought me a cold cola drink. "Drink it up, it'll settle your tummy," Nana said.

There was a sudden rush of checking the time, gathering up of hand luggage and then it was time for Piloo to leave. I'd always shut her out, joked with Rita about her, but maybe she wasn't so bad. I nearly held on to her hand and I nearly said, "Don't go! Come with us!" I nearly started to cry.

VeeVee, our teacher, has a favourite saying. "*Too late. The saddest words in the English language,*" she pronounces in a doomy voice. Maybe I'd never see Piloo again! Sweat evaporated, leaving me feeling cold and exposed. But then Piloo was gone and there I was with my grandfather and, even worse, with myself.

There were only two kinds of autos: a little dinky one called Maruti and ours, the grandly named Ambassador, which was lumbering and old-fashioned. "The very best for our potholed roads," Nana said.

Jeevan kept it spotless inside and polished to a saleroom finish outside. On the back shelf a Thermos flask moved like a rolling pin next to a black umbrella and a neatly folded newspaper. My grandfather sat in front with Jeevan, his arm resting along the back of the seat. I saw with a shock how thin it was, showing sticking-out blue veins. He was old and frail and it occurred to me that he was coming to the end of his life. I brushed away the knowledge that he would die one day. Suddenly it seemed possible that Rita might die; and Piloo, too, in a plane crash. To stop my morbid imaginings, I breathed deeply and pulled myself together by biting my lip and focusing on the scenery. Thankfully my grandfather started up a conversation.

"Have you read *Kim* by Rudyard Kipling?" He turned round to look at me.

"This is the famous Grand Trunk Road, which Kim travelled with the old lama. Little Friend of all the World," he chuckled. "It's my favourite novel."

I didn't know any Kipling except for "If", and I quoted the few lines I could remember. VeeVee had made us memorize the whole poem.

"If you can keep your head when all about you
Are losing theirs and blaming it on you;
If you can trust yourself when all men doubt you,
But make allowance for their doubting too;
If you can wait and not be tired by waiting,
Or, being lied about, don't deal in lies,
Or being hated, don't give way to hating,
And ... and ... and ... yet..."

Nana was delighted to discover that I wasn't a complete airhead. He nodded in time to my recitation and finished the verse for me, "And yet don't look too good, nor talk too wise." He beamed. "*Shabash!* That means congratulations!"

The Grand Trunk Road was narrow for a major highway and very bumpy. Jeevan kept pulling up behind bullock carts piled high with sugarcane and clumsy black bicycles each with two or three passengers, including at least one baby. Country people straggled along the roadside thwacking buffaloes that looked as heavy and smug as the businessmen at the airport. Sometimes we were shaded from the blazing sun by avenues of trees, but mostly the flat plains stretched on either side of the road and the light was so dazzling it hurt my eyes. Enormous bull-nosed lorries thundered by, belching black exhaust fumes in their wake. They were painted in brilliant colours and all of them had a cheery "OK", "Tata" and "Horn Please" for good measure written across the back.

And now, more than six hours after leaving New Delhi, we were climbing up the foothills of the Himalaya, the air starting to become cooler. I rolled down the window and breathed deeply. Pine trees and rocks and deep gullies. The road wound higher and higher, and I was getting further and further away from home.

"Not far to go now." We were stretching our legs by a roadside tea stall where the tea came in little ribbed glasses, hot and very sweet. "Daroga used to be a British cantonment. There's an army hospital and in the old days soldiers were sent there for a rest ... usually if they'd gone a bit funny in the head." Nana smiled, tapping his temple. "I was stationed there when I was a young soldier and I decided I'd buy a house and live in Daroga after I retired from the army."

"Do you still grow mushrooms?" I asked, remembering this from my last visit.

"Yes, but not to sell. I sold off the mushroom farm last year to another ex-army chap. Now it's all golf, bridge and my orchids. Oh, and a new passion: I'm writing a book on military history." My heart sank a little. What did I know about golf, bridge and orchids? Maybe Ma was right – what would I do all day?

The road climbed higher and higher and there was very little traffic now. Bicycles would need thirty gears to keep going. A goatherd trudged up-hill, one arm folded behind, the other brandishing a switch at his herd. I approved of the way the mountains showed their secrets, a sudden trickle of water through rocks, the hot smell of wild flowers and pine trees towering on all sides like guardians.

There was a mysteriousness about the mountains that was new and exciting. It was such a relief to leave the plains behind, dusty, exposed and endless. Now the sun had disappeared behind the heights leaving a smoky blue twilight and the journey was coming to an end.

"Here we are, the suburbs of Daroga."

I realized my grandfather was joking, when a few houses appeared round the corner, small and poor-looking and perched on the edge of the grassy, rocky ravine that fell away from the side of the road. The town itself was very small and we drove through the central bazaar, past more houses hidden behind stone walls, a temple, a church all boarded up, a hospital and a school with a sign "The Convent of the Immaculate Conception". Ma's old school! We passed the famous convent where Rita and Piloo had been boarders and learned that ghastly dialect that Ma still remembered. The church looked just like a country church in England, but the grave-stones leaned, tangled over with nettles and creep-ers and the gate had collapsed on its hinges.

Then Jeevan changed into first gear and took the car up a narrow lane and pulled up in front of a long white cross-barred gate. A sign saying "Stoneleigh" hung on it. Jeevan blew the horn and a girl came running to open it. A black and white sheepdog ran alongside the car. They must have had a guard once who sat in a little hut by the side of the gate, but it was now empty.

"That's Bina, Hira and Lila's granddaughter. Did Rita tell you about her? She was away the last time you visited. She is like a second grandchild – a very bright girl, a couple of years older than you."

There'd been no time for more than a glimpse of Bina when, with a scrunching of gravel, the car stopped in front of a low stone house, with the verandah that I remembered, and there was my nani on the steps, her arms wide open and a smile that stretched from ear to ear.

"Darling! How lovely to see you at last. It's been too long. Did you have a good journey? Was it terribly hot down there? You must be exhausted."

I was gripped by a bear hug, surprisingly powerful from someone who looked like she might blow away any minute. I felt massive beside her and Nana in my jeans and clumpy trainers. Then I was hugged by Hira and Lila. Lila seemed overcome with emotion and kept dabbing her eyes with the end of her sari. Last of all Bina came forward to say hello. She was a couple of inches taller than me and very pretty, with a long, neat pigtail down her back.

"Welcome to Daroga, Sarla-*didi*."

The darkness was quickly blotting out the garden

and the mountains beyond. I had been drowning in tiredness but even though my eyes were stinging, I came alive again. I wanted to see everything, to rush out and explore, but I was led into the sitting room where logs were burning in the fireplace. On the high mantel were silver-framed photographs, one of Rita looking like a gipsy with a flower behind her ear, Nana in uniform, Nani presenting a sports trophy, me as a baby, me at two, at four, at five and six. It was very strange seeing myself everywhere.

We had buttered toast with jam and lots of tea. Hira and Lila kept calling me "Baby" and everyone was fussing, asking me if I wanted anything else. "Milkshake, Baby? Rumble-tumble eggs? Ice-cream and meringues?" Lila stroked my hair, Nani held my hand (the hand that wasn't shovelling food into my mouth). Nana smiled and smiled his pleasure.

There was a lump in my throat because I felt so terribly happy. I wasn't used to being showered with so much love and attention. Then they took me to my room and I fell asleep almost at once and didn't wake up until lunchtime the next day.

Five

SARLA

Snug as a bug in a rug. A-bug-in-a-rug, a-cat-in-a-hat, a-foot-in-a-boot, a-girl-in-a … in a what? Curl? Furl? I juggled a few rhymes in my head and stretched luxuriously between the crisp cotton sheets, safe under the warm quilt, a quiver of light sneaking through a crack in the curtains. Snug and smug. Someone had tiptoed in while I was asleep and left a glass of fresh orange juice on my bedside table. I felt happy and light and carefree. Something like joyful expectation ran up all the way from my toes, up my legs to the top of my head. No school, no homework, no stress about being cool and on top of things. All that was another world. I felt as free as free could be.

I turned my ankles from side to side and wriggled my toes in a sort of ecstasy of laziness. Even Rita had faded into the background for the time being. *No worries* … all I had to do was be myself, minus my normal smart alec front. I had to admit that only four days after arriving, the novelty of swanning around like a star was getting a tiny bit tiresome. Everyone's eyes on me, all the time! The gardener, the driver, the laundryman, the bread man who came round with a steel trunk, full of buns, cream horns and bread, strapped to his bike − all watching me like I was a character in a TV sitcom! Even Carmen the dog followed me everywhere with her eyes.

Hira and Lila talked to me in this peculiar way, not quite a coo, but like they were indulging a baby − or an imbecile, or someone handicapped − and I was beginning to crave a tiny bit of abrasion, a bit of argument, friction.

"Come, Baby, try this; no leave that chapatti, take this one just made, all puffed up and piping hot!"

"Which dessert? Queen of puddings made with our own raspberry jam; banana fritters; or spun sugar baskets filled with candied cape gooseberries and whipped cream; or lemon pancakes…"

So much choice! The *Looks* diet had to be forced to the back-burner. Not that it took much forcing.

Never before had I been caressed and touched as much. Lila stroked my hair and held my hand whenever she got the chance, and Nani hugged me and draped her arm round my shoulder. Nana listened attentively like I was the Wise Woman of West London. It was all getting a bit much, especially as there was another pair of eyes watching beadily from a pile of homework.

I couldn't figure out Bina. It wasn't that I disliked her, but she was rather strange. I'd never known anyone who did nothing but swot, swot, swot all day. Straight home from school, she slid behind her desk, busy, busy, busy, calibrating angles with a compass, rocking forward and backwards like a mullah memorizing the Quran, and scribbling essays in her nerdy way. But her most irritating habit was the way she sidled up to my nana. "Uncleji, please check..." sucking a pencil, making peculiar sideways nods with that earnest expression that said, I'm so good, I'm drinking in every word. Ugghhh!

I guessed that she didn't think much of me (her opposite in every possible way) from the disapproving glances she sent. I must have got on her nerves: my loud guffaw, my untidy hair, plus the fact that I was flavour of the month. Lila must have told her about the contents of my suitcase. As Bina's granny had picked up each pair of grungy jeans and leggings she let out a long-suffering sigh, "Hey Ram," or "Dear God."

I'd quickly realized that this part of the world was, sartorially, very different from my patch in London. Everyone looked neat and clean, wearing matching outfits, not one hair out of place. Nani and Lila's dress sense was completely different from Rita's. Nani wore exquisite, beautifully ironed silk saris (pale pink, grey or turquoise matched with dainty blouses) well cut "slacks" (as she called trousers), pearl studs with a single strand round her neck. A perfectly draped cardigan hung from her shoulders, the sleeves empty – very *Tatler* – and on her feet she wore soft moccasins made by Ho-Lee the Chinese shoemaker of Daroga.

"For years we were lucky enough to have skilful Chinese cobblers in every hill station, but their sons are emigrating to Australia. Ho-Lee is one of the last. He used to make me silver high-heeled sandals for our army mess dances."

She adjusted her expression to seem carefree and un-bossy, even though she was about to tell me what to do. "Sarla, now that you are in India, it might be fun to try a smart salwar kameez suit? We have quite a good tailor in the bazaar. Let's go shopping!"

All this was conveyed in a light-hearted sort of way, because I guessed she had made up her mind to be my dress saviour. Who knows, maybe she'd been lying in bed worrying about it. I'm sure she didn't fancy being pointed out as the grandmother of the freakish girl from London. What would her friends say! Lila, who changed into a fresh cotton sari each day and moved about nimbly in Bata trainers and woollen socks, held up a pair of distressed jeans, cut at the knees, and wailed, "Koshyji!"

"Never, never, never, Nani! You'll never get me to look girly. I have my own style. Everyone in London dresses like this!" (This was stretching the truth somewhat, but I didn't want my carefully composed persona interfered with.) There were a couple more "Hey Rams" from Lila, who had unearthed more disasters.

"Who says salwar kameez is girly? Depends on the cut, of course; it's a pair of harem pants with a tunic on top – so ethnic and practical! Just like trousers, but a little more dressy, if you like. I thought you were an adventurous type – you know, when in Rome-kind-of-thing… What do you say?"

I felt thunder tracks revving up between my eyebrows.

"Come on! Let's get a pair or two made up by Misrilal. You don't have to wear it if you hate it. That's a deal." She trying her best to "buck me up", in her words; I was supposed to play it like *Sarla: the Pluckiest Girl in the Fourth Form.*

Oh well, I reasoned, it wouldn't kill me to make my Nani happy. So tactfully had she glided from characteristic enthusiasm to near surrender, that I felt a bit of a meanie. Things like compromise, or give and take, were never my strong point, but I quickly thought of a face-saver, for her and myself. "OK, OK, you win, Nani – but if I put on that fancy dress can I have new shoes to go with it?"

I know it was inconsistent, because I really, *really* wasn't up for a big shopping trip, but for some perverse reason I'd been coveting platform heels. The thought of looking two inches taller than my five foot two sent a delicious frisson through me, *especially* as Rita would never have allowed tarty footwear.

Nani brightened. She didn't have a clue about my thinking process. "Of course, sweetheart, if that's what you want. We'll go on Saturday and take Bina with us. She needs a break from her revision."

Daroga bazaar was only half a mile downhill, but it would have meant carrying back parcels uphill, or being towed by a sweating rickshaw man, so we had the creepy Jeevan drive us to the shops and park near the arcade. Looking back, it had been surprisingly easy to get used to a chauffeur, a cook, a maid and a gardener! Even though Hira and Lila felt like family, and were always treated as such by my grandparents, they were still their employees. They worked hard and I'm sure they were fairly paid, but we just sat back and took them for granted.

"Your Nana's probably told you about Daroga. See, there are the old barracks for the ordinary tommies. The British officers lived in bungalows like ours on this side of the Ridge, which is the posh part."

"The Chestnuts, Sunnyside, The Gables," I recited as we went by at a snail's pace. Nani hated going fast, but basically the Ambassador was a lumberer, though Jeevan had already shown off his natural driving style (accelerate, overtake, honk furiously, brake suddenly) on our way from Delhi to Daroga.

"Over the Ridge, in that direction, is The Retreat where our friend the princess stays in her summer palace, and if you look the other way you'll see the convent where Rita went to school. The waiting list for the boarding school just grows longer: girls come from the States, Canada, New Zealand, the UK – from Indian families who've settled abroad. Some parents put down their babies' names as soon as they're born! We're very lucky to live here: nice people, good climate, golf, walks." She sounded very contented.

Nani took Bina's right hand and my left and

we strolled towards the shops in the arcade. The bazaar was further down the hill.

"What or who is Colenol Barrow?" I asked.

Nani laughed. "Oh, those sign painters! It's meant to be Colonel Barrow, who used to be the commanding officer a long time ago. The Municipal Committee renamed it Mahatma Gandhi Road, but they still haven't got used to the new name, twenty years later."

We walked past Duli Ram chemist, Snow White dry-cleaners and then I saw Bata shoe shop. "Don't forget my shoes, Nani – you promised!"

A shoeshine boy, with a neat stack of tins and brushes, was giving a mirror shine to a shoe perched on a stand while his client, balancing on one foot, looked over his shoulder listening to something on the radio that had drawn a crowd of men. There were about twenty of them, muffled up in woollen scarves and balaclavas, gathered round a transistor that was conveying a crackly and urgent-sounding commentary in Hindi.

"I didn't know there was a test match on," Nani observed. We perched on stools inside Bata and waited for someone to serve us, but all the assistants were on the verandah listening with rapt attention. "Can't be a test match. Maybe someone died. Bina, go and find out what's happened."

Bina managed to attract the manager's attention and there was a flurry of activity as the assistants came scurrying in full of apologies.

"Oho, Madamji, so sorry, so sorry. We are just hearing about the Liberation Front boys. Some fresh news is coming in from the trial."

"Are they a pop group, Nani?"

Bina eyes widened. She grimaced. "Don't be so silly, Sarla. A *pop group*!"

Nani explained. "No, sweetie. We are talking about a dangerous group of Maoist guerrilla fighters who have been on the run from the police, ever since they kidnapped an Oxfam worker in the mountains. I think they must have caught some of the gang." She looked questioningly at the Bata manager, who nodded vigorously.

"Yes, Madamji. Five were caught and we have been listening to the result of the trial. They have been immediately sentenced to ten years each under POTA, Prevention of Terrorism Act. Interview with the police chief and all. All in Daroga who have family in villages are worried about nears and dears. Now we can sleep happy and cosy in our beds. For the information of our Baby – Madamji, these boys are all out for separate hill state with our own language and assembly. They are daggers drawn with central gorement" – he meant government, I think – "but Liberation boys are hot-bloods. They like to kidnap, set off bombs and so forth. Now no worries, at least for some time! Now, baby-Madam, what can I fetch you?"

Assistants scampered up and down ladders fetching boxes of shoes until I chose the tartiest of them all: red strappy sandals with gold-coloured platforms. That would show Rita! I wanted them partly as a joke, because I so much looked forward to seeing her face when I wore them.

Nani was horrified, of course, but sporting enough not to question my taste – or lack of it; however, I didn't miss the faintly disgusted look that passed over Bina's face when Nani wrote out the cheque.

I tried to find out more about the Liberation Front, which had the romantic ring of Che Guevara's army. "Tell me some more, Nani. Are people really frightened?"

"Hard to find out the truth. Yes and no. Most village people are hand in glove with the Liberation Front because they feel at last someone is siding with them. They feed and shelter the guerrillas and lead the police on wild goose chases. I don't think those boys will ever get their way, especially now the government has decided to send in army units to hunt them down. In some ways they are like the old bandits, or dacoits, but with political ambitions."

A look passed between her and Bina. "But Auntyji, the Liberation Front only wants people to get what they should have by law. They are asking for a fair deal. Don't you think they are the voice of the people?"

She would have said more, but I had just seen something incredible, which made me start to laugh. We were walking away from the arcade towards an enormous cinema hoarding advertising a film called *Boyfriend*. The heroine was painted in fleshy pink colours with eyes swimming in tears. Her huge, cone-shaped boobs were pointing at a space roughly around the hero's left eyebrow with enough cleavage to drive a couple of tractors through. It was so grotesque and kitsch that my eyes nearly popped out. And then the hiccups started because I was laughing so much.

"Stop it, Sarla," Bina scolded. "People are looking at you! What is so funny about Indian films? I bet you've never even seen a Hindi movie, so who are you to cut jokes about them?"

How was I supposed to know that I was making fun of her favourite Bollywood stars? My laughing stopped at her acid tone. So Miss Goody Two-Shoes did have a voice of her own, which was a surprise, but not an entirely uncomfortable one. Here was the friction that I'd been missing! So she didn't like me, otherwise she wouldn't have been so sharp. She'd probably labelled me a stuck-up, arrogant know-it-all. Fine. She was welcome to her opinion, even though I didn't like being judged like this. It wasn't fair.

But I was quickly diverted by the sights and sounds of the bazaar. The tinny tinkle of bike bells; the clang of temple bells; a seller of spicy snacks ringing his handbell; rubber horns pressed by rickshawmen as they weaved their way through the crowds; far-off klaxons on long-distance lorries; people shouting friendly greetings and angry curses; beggars whining, dogs barking; music blaring from shops, even crows cawing perched on an electric cable.

Nani held up a warning finger so I wouldn't splash into cowpats, slushy rubbish and pools of stagnant water. We were walking along a lane that got narrower and narrower. Tiny open-fronted shops lined it on both sides: I saw Ho-Lee the shoe-maker; a Chinese dentist with a poster of gummy fangs over the entrance; fruit and vegetables piled high in shining heaps of red and green and orange; the sweet maker on his haunches piping something into a blackened pan, then lifting out golden-coloured spirals of a sweet called *jalebi*. I smelt a powerful mixture of piss and rotten vegetation, sweat and jasmine and things frying. Most of all I caught Bina's watchful eyes taking note of my reaction to the foreign squalor all around us.

The smell was terrible. I had to cover my nose and breathe through my mouth, and when I felt something wet and soft at my bare elbow I screamed. A lean white cow had sidled up and was butting my behind. Bits of green vegetation trailed from its mouth. Since I had nothing to offer, it moved on dipping into shopkeepers' lunches, lifting apples from the fruit seller's barrow, pulling a long white radish from a basket outside the vegetable shop. It stopped outside the shop of Seth Sitaram, ALL KINDS OF FANCY CLOTH AND MATERIAL, as if it were weighing up its chances.

We squeezed our way past its bony frame into the doorway and the owner of the shop greeted us like long lost friends. He bowed and did many *namastes*.

"Please, make yourself at home," he said with extravagant warmth. He settled us on a wooden bench in front of a mattress covered with a white sheet. "Pepsi? Fanta? Chai?" Seth Sitaram looked at us expectantly, but the cow was restless. It gobbled up a garland of yellow marigolds that was draped over a small statue of a goddess. Then Seth begged us to have patience, leant back and produced a paper bag of round yellow sweetmeats from a shelf behind the cash register, which were tenderly fed to the animal. "Cow is mother, cow is friend; everyday she comes. It's my duty to be kind to her," he explained.

I'd heard about Indian holy cows, but this was the first time I'd seen what they were about. Nani explained afterwards that Hindus didn't eat beef, because the cow represented all kinds of special things to them. But I did wonder why the poor thing was so hungry and thin and why she hadn't been washed for a very long time.

Bina and Nani ignored her and the cow ambled away. Then business began in earnest as Seth Sitaram started to show off his treasures: bales and bales of different cottons and silks and velvets and fabrics that I couldn't name. He threw down each bale of cloth with a flourish and jerked out a length to let us feel it properly, which Bina and Nani did, holding a bit with thumb and finger, rubbing it, crushing it, rejecting it with a shake of their heads and moving on to the next one.

Bina picked up a dark green silk patterned with small yellow roses. She held it against me.

"Nothing doing!" I growled.

It came out abrupt and unfriendly, and to my horror I saw Bina's eyes fill with tears. I would have done anything to play that scene again. I bit my lip, not knowing how to make up. I was so used to saying whatever came to the tip of my tongue. A little too late I explained, "That print just isn't my style," but Bina was staring out into the lane ignoring me.

"Something nice and plain in cotton for Sarla," Nani told the shopkeeper. "And why don't you cut three and a half metres for a suit of that green silk for Bina? I want to give her a little present for all the studying she's been doing." She had picked up the tension between us and was trying to make it all better.

In the end I came away with black and red cotton, perfectly plain, and after thanking the Seth we made our way to "Misrilal Tailor", only a few shops down the squelchy lane.

Well, that's that, I thought. I felt a bit depressed. Even though I'd sidestepped the cowpats, I'd put my foot in it. I felt very foreign, very much an outsider, a new girl. I didn't understand the language, the way Indians thought, their behaviour, what they expected of me. I felt awkward and clumsy and stupid. It was the second time in a week that I wished I could go back home.

A dummy dressed in a brown felt hat and blazer stood guard over Misrilal Tailor shop. Its hat hung at a rakish angle over one painted eye and it had a red bow mouth with its top teeth showing. It was comic, but I dared not laugh at it. A rather obscene display of sari blouses hung from a rack with sticking out boobs. Why were so many bosoms on display – first the poster and now these bustier things – when real women went around covering their chests with dupattas, or scarves, their eyes fixed on the ground?

The tailor, Misrilal, took his job very seriously, not smiling even once as he measured Bina and me and barked out our vital statistics to an assistant, who wrote it all in a notebook. The tailor snipped a fragment of my chosen cloth and pinned it to my measurements in the notebook and did the same with Bina's green silk, so there would be no confusion about what was meant for whom.

"Make it fit well here," Bina told him, indicating her chest region.

"With darts, or princess cut?"

"What is the latest fashion in Delhi?"

"Princess cut."

"Then shape it properly under the arms – no loose folds, please."

This is where the difference in our ages showed. Bina wanted her kameez shaped to flatter her figure and I wished my sprouting boobs would disappear. "I just want mine straight up and down, like a shirt," I told Misrilal.

Our shopping done, we walked back to the car

and I saw Jeevan from a distance puffing a ciga-rette, which he threw down and ground under his winkle-pickers when he saw us coming. Next to our boxy white Ambassador was a swanky grey Bentley whose number plate read HHD 1.

"Her Highness Daroga," Nani explained. "That's our friend Vidya's car – you know, the princess I told you about. We play a lot of golf as well as bridge." Then in a lower tone, "Here she comes – she is quite a character so don't get shocked."

An apparition rolled toward us, hand raised in a kind of salute.

"Oho, Koshy! Rita's brat?" A rotund woman of about seventy, wearing bright red cord trousers under a stripy top, chucked me under my chin and looked me over critically. "Ha, a chip off the old block, I see! Fiery and independent, if I'm not mistaken. A modern miss! It's Sarla, isn't it? Well, Sarla, what do you think of our Bharat, that is India, eh?"

She had a deafening voice that rolled up from somewhere deep inside her Michelin tummy. I wanted to say, "Dirty, smelly and full of staring eyes and bullies like you," but I mumbled something like "Very interesting."

"I don't suppose your mother has taught you any-thing about your heritage. India is an ancient civili-zation, a great culture. Our love for our motherland will never die! Never mind, we'll educate you, won't we, Koshy?" She let out a great wheezing smoker's laugh. Was she taking a swipe at my mum? "Oh, I mustn't forget my manners." She gestured at her companion, a tall handsome boy of about eighteen or nineteen. "This is my nephew, Sidhartha, but we call him Dinkoo. Ask him to take you around Daroga – he knows it like the back of his hand. As you can see, he's handsome, but also charming and clever."

I was instantly smitten. What amazing grey eyes! What a great smile! But *Dinkoo*? His ghastly aunt turned her attention to Bina. "And Bina. You are well, aren't you? Slogging away? Get your First and join Dinkoo at Medical College in Chandigarh." Finally, wagging her forefinger at Nani, "Bye, my dear. See you on the course on Thursday as usual. Bring Sarla; she can walk with us." With a final wave she heaved herself into her Bentley, having chucked her shopping bags at the chauffeur, and they sailed off.

Nani was smiling. "What did I tell you?"

We got into our car and I noticed that Bina was flustered. Her eyes were unusually bright, and it wasn't because she'd been crying.

"Princess Vidya's father, the old maharajah, was larger than life. He had to give up his kingdom when India became independent from the British Raj. All the maharajahs and princes − and there were more than five hundred of them − were absolute dictators in their kingdoms. Now they can't use their titles − they're plain Shri or Mister − but Vidya hasn't quite come to terms with the modern world. Did you notice that she didn't invite Bina with you to the club on Thursday? I'm afraid she is a terrible snob, but we make allowances for her. Everyone's sorted out in social compartments. She'll only mix with the 'top drawer'. In India people call it the 'creamy layer': you know, crème de la crème! Bina's used to her, aren't you, *bittia*?"

Bina's smile was a little forced. I saw her folding a piece of paper into smaller and smaller pieces on her knee. I wondered if she had been given a love letter, and if that was the reason for her bright eyes and air of distraction.

We got back home for chocolate cake and tea by the fire. It got dark very early, by five thirty, and mist was rolling down the mountains even though it was summer. From the window I saw little pricks of light on the opposite hills.

Hira brought in extra hot water for the teapot. "You like bazaar, Baby? Nice shops like London? Make friends with Bina and teach her good English, for getting high marks in exam!"

"Where is the child?" Nana asked. "Sarla, go and call her for her tea. She wanted help her with her maths, and now she's disappeared."

Six

Himalayan nights are cold, even in summer. Stars dense as sand on a beach blaze till daybreak; white light from the full moon shines almost as bright as sunlight. It feels uncanny, not right: the shadows too black; the light too bright; the whooo-whoooo *of the owl sinister; the sounds in the pine forest too loud; familiar things exaggerated and spooky.*

On the outskirts of a mountain village, about a day's journey from Daroga, a young man was sleeping under the night sky. His eyes had closed as he'd kept watch for his friends, who were collapsed from exhaustion inside a shepherd's hut roofed with turves. The hut was well camouflaged from the mountain road. The army patrol searching for guerrillas would have found them only if they had been led to the hut by a goatherd.

The patrol tramped on northwards following a tip-off, and the sleeper stirred in his nightmares, for now safe from capture.

The young man dreamed of an ancient fort, built into a rocky hillside in another land far from the mountains, another climate where a deadly sun burned man and beast into submission. He saw a small boy running ahead of his shadow, dodging from scrub to scrub, hugging the ground until he reached the summit. He saw a woman dressed in men's clothes, a gun slung on her back. She ruffled the boy's hair. She took a bundle of supplies from his hands and scanned a note that he passed to her. He saw anger darken her face, heard her cry, "Betrayed!"

Horrified, he watched as she crossed over to the ramparts of the fort and dug the rifle barrel into the ribs of the man at the lookout post. She fired and then fired again many times.

The watchman heard the boy's heart go thump-thump *as he fled to hide under the tomb of the long-dead princess who had been killed defending the same fort six hundred years before. He was shaking with fright. He quickly flattened himself on the ground when a army of policemen arrived and the terrible slaughter began. He saw his father killed – the shot leaving a black hole between his eyes – and the woman being taken away by the police. They led her like an animal to the slaughterhouse, a rope round her neck. She was bloody, her teeth broken, her mouth red, long hair wild like the goddess Kali. The boy hid until everyone had gone, long after the night was old.*

Afterwards he picked his way through the ghosts, the pools of spilled blood and scattered belongings of the robber gang.

He couldn't see straight and he stepped on a watch that had belonged to his father. He stumbled back home to his village and didn't speak for many weeks.

The watchman woke chilled, but sweating. He stretched his stiff limbs. His hair was slick from dew. It was a familiar dream – one that often visited him. He sat thinking, motionless, until his companions stumbled out of the hut, yawning and rubbing their eyes. There were five men altogether, and the youngest was hardly more than fifteen. Their uniforms of khaki cotton shirts and trousers were crumpled and filthy, their boots were old and down at heel. They looked as if they hadn't eaten properly for weeks.

"How long will it take to get to Purulia?"

The watchman, their leader, answered, "Four days if we find a jeep to hijack."

"Are you sure the arms and ammunition are coming from Europe and not Afghanistan? We need good new guns and not some leftover rubbish from the Russian war."

"Don't worry, it is good stuff, the best. Our Naxalite comrades in Bihar will teach us how to fire the weapons and make these new-style bombs, and then we'll come back and teach our comrades in the mountains."

The leader snapped them to attention. "Let's get on. We have to find food in the village before pushing off."

The five young men of the Liberation Front scrambled down the mountainside and struck the feeder road where the army patrol had passed just hours before. They regrouped in military fashion and walked to Rewari village where they would be sure to be given refreshment before their long journey east.

They were heading for Purulia near the Nepalese border, where a plane-load of guns and ammunition was scheduled to parachute down fresh supplies of weapons into the jungle. The Liberation Front had been told a range of dates when they should show up to collect their share of the bounty. The leader of the group from Rewari village was responsible for bringing their share back safely to their boss, the comrade-in-chief of the Liberation Front.

Seven

❧

BINA

I stared at the crumpled piece of exercise paper in my hand without really seeing it. My vision was blurry and my thoughts came and went, crazily crashing into one another. What was I going to do? Who would help me? I felt overwhelmed by helplessness.

"Meet me in the carport after we get home. Urgent," read the Hindi words.

Jeevan had thrust the note into my hand just before we started home after our shopping trip. This was the last thing I could cope with. I was already feeling annoyed and irritated with Sarla: so ignorant of simple things, a spoiled little girl from England, sniggering at our ways, wanting quick answers to silly questions. How was I going to keep my patience for the next six weeks? *Rabba*, oh God,

I prayed. I just wanted to get home to my maths and bury myself in my revision. But first I had to deal with Jeevan.

While the others were having tea I managed to slip away. Suddenly Jeevan stepped out of the shadows and grabbed my arm. He squeezed till it hurt and whispered, "I told you the deadline is today. Why haven't you answered me? Why? Why?" With each "why" he squeezed tighter. "Don't forget I can change your life, just like that," he clicked his fingers. "I thought you would come to your senses. I thought you'd be desperate not to have a scandal. Don't care about your good name? No self-respect even?"

He knew full well that he was playing to an Indian girl's fear of social disgrace. There isn't much forgiveness in these parts.

"I know I can make you happy. Bina, you know I'm crazy about you, so this is your last chance to save yourself!" Like all men, putting the responsibility on the girl. "Otherwise I don't have a choice. I'll go to your school and tell them about your mother, tell them who you really are. If you haven't become engaged to me by the end of the month I will really do it. Yes I will. Don't cry, there's nothing to cry about. We'll be very happy together. You understand?"

He pulled my plait and then stroked my cheek. The man was a brute. I could smell his disgusting breath all over me. I managed to shake him off.

"Get off me, you animal."

He just grinned, in a lazy sort of way that I could tell was copied from the film star Shahrukh Khan. He threatened me with a mocking finger before melting back into the dark.

Ugh, how dirty he made me feel. Bit by bit my anger grew – how dare he do that to me? How dare he think he had any claims over me?

I rubbed my arm where it hurt. There would be bruises tomorrow. Then, overcome by the seriousness of the situation, I collapsed on the steps that led to the verandah, my head in my arms.

I love watching movies where the heroine has to struggle with some awful situation: her man has been killed, or has disappeared; her mother-in-law has thrown her out of the house with her baby in her arms; she's abandoned in a dark and lonely place and sits sobbing her heart out. I had read in film magazines that they put glycerine in her eyes to bring on fake tears. But my tears were real and I wasn't acting in some Bollywood film. I had to stifle the noise of my crying in case someone heard me inside the house. Someone was calling my name, then I heard footsteps so I quickly wiped my nose, keeping my head down; how was I going to face anyone? An arm came to rest on my shoulders.

"Bina, Bina, why are you crying? Listen, I'm really sorry I was a bit rude this afternoon. Honestly, I didn't mean it. It's just the way I talk – you mustn't take it seriously. Come inside and have some chocolate cake…" Sarla pulled my sleeve. She must have thought I was sulking.

"You are just a stupid ignorant *git-mit* idiot from abroad. What do you know about anything? You come here with your proudy ways and think you're better than us?" My face was burning; when I lose my temper, I really lose it! I carried on, "Shut up, shut up, go away and leave me alone!" I learned to say shut up from films as well, but I had never dared say it before.

I shocked myself by this venomous outburst. Sarla's arm stayed where she had put it. I thought she would have flounced off. When I was younger I watched other, socially confident girls at school carelessly breaking and making friendships. They'd stick their thumb behind their upper front teeth, jerk it out and hiss, "*Kutti kutti kutti*," meaning I'm breaking with you for ever. I thought maybe Sarla will do that; angry with my rejection, she'd tattle to the others that I was in a bad mood, crying on the steps; that she'd tried her best but couldn't get me to come into the house.

To my astonishment she didn't go away, and after a short while I heard her whisper, "I said I was sorry."

"What's sorry got to do with anything?" I almost shouted. "You are just a tourist. I have to live with all my awful problems." I couldn't help going on. I should have kept my mouth shut, but what I'd said was live bait for Sarla's curiosity.

"Problems, what problems? Maybe I can help you, Bina…"

"Huh, you'll never understand. Here today, gone tomorrow…" I said bitterly.

"Hey, never mind, don't say anything now. Go and wash your eyes with cold water." Her voice was very gentle and sweet.

My eyes filled up again. When I let out my real feelings it's like a dam has burst. I can either cry, or get angry, nothing in between.

"Hush, hush. Tell me what's happened. It can't be that bad."

"It is worse than bad, you'll never understand!"

I felt her grip tighten. "Don't say you're pregnant! Are you?" I glanced at her; her eyes were round like Ping-Pong balls.

Horrified, I – who have never even held a boy's

hand – gave out a little shriek. "What are you saying? That is the dirtiest, filthiest, most *shameful* thing to say to me! Oh my God, you have no idea about anything."

"OK, OK, I've made a mistake, but lots of girls your age get pregnant in England. It's not always their fault. So why don't you tell me what's wrong then?"

My mind flipped to the sitting room inside. What would Koshy Aunty and Uncleji be thinking? What would my grandparents say if they saw me like this? I had to do something quickly to keep face. I got up, elbowing her to one side.

"Some other time. I have to go now. Say you couldn't find me. They'll think I went home to fetch some books or something. Tell them what you like, but don't you *dare* say I was crying!" Once I was up I felt a bit more in control.

"I'll cover for you only if you tell me the truth. Promise you will?"

"All *right*. Now go back – no blabbing."

I gave her a little push towards the steps and ran to the little gate that opened on to the path leading to the back of Stoneleigh and my grandparents' house.

Carmen, who had been sitting at my feet whining, got to her feet and trotted after me and I was very glad of her company in the darkness. She was no friend of Jeevan. She only had to bare her teeth for that coward to back off.

Eight

❧

SARLA

I wriggled into the tunic part of the outfit, since it only had a neck opening without zips or buttons, and pulled on the salwar. Only four days after being measured, Misrilal's boy had brought our new clothes to Stoneleigh on his bike, nicely wrapped and ironed.

I hardly recognized myself in the long mirror. The baggy black pants and red kameez looked so grown-up and stylish. I twirled this way then that way, slipped on the tarty platforms and strutted around. I pouted at my reflection and stuck out my hips, walking in a pigeon-toed goose-step like a model and nearly tripping over my face.

Lila walked in with a pile of clean towels over her arm. She covered her mouth with her hand and said, "Baby, very nice. *Bahut accha!* Koshyji, look at our Baby."

Everyone made a huge fuss, telling me I looked amazing.

Nani said, "I told you, didn't I? Now let's get another set made since this is such a success. Aren't they more comfortable?"

It was true – no rigid seams digging into my flesh, no tight waistband, no wondering if my bum looked enormous – Indian clothes were really flattering.

The next day was my grandparents' golfing afternoon, and I was going to walk round the course with them while Bina did her "swotting". It would have been more fun if she had come with us, but she seemed determined to finish some very boring-looking maths homework. I wondered if that was a convenient excuse for not having to explain the other night's scene, but she was so unbending that I gave up trying to persuade her.

A slight movement under the verandah caught my eye. I checked to see whether it was the gardener but saw Jeevan flattened up against the wall, watching Bina through the window. There was a really unpleasant, hungry sort of look on his face. Was he spying, stalking her like people did when they had an obsession? Maybe *he* was the reason she'd been crying. I had to find a chance to talk to her in private. There was much more to her than I'd realized. The nerdy side was a front. Then I remembered Rita had mentioned she was a "funny little thing" and made up my mind to find out what made her tick.

As we were being driven to the golf club, Nani drew me closer in a warm hug. "Oh, Sarla, you can't imagine how much I've longed for you to be with us. Now you have to tell me all about your life in England. I'm just bursting with questions. This may sound very rude, but are you one of those 'latchkey children' that one reads about?"

I shrugged instead of answering. She probed further. "I suppose you and Rita eat together when she's home from work and manages to cook a nice meal?"

This cosy picture was so far from the truth that I couldn't help snorting, which quickly changed to a cough. *Rita cook a nice meal!* Sure. She did manage to heat up pizzas quite effectively in the microwave. *I'm not going to tell tales*, I thought. If Nani didn't have a clue about how we lived, it was better left that way.

I tried to change the subject by talking about Bina, which nearly resulted in blurting out my suspicions about her stalker. I braked just in time. Lowering my voice I asked, "Nani, tell me about Bina. She's not easy, is she, and I don't think she likes me much."

Nana turned round from the front passenger seat. "Aha, but do you like her? Poor Bina has had a tough life."

Nani added, "Ask her to take you to school with her one day. You'll get a better idea of how difficult things are for her socially, and you'll have something to talk about."

Did Jeevan understand English? Probably not. Surely Nana and Nani wouldn't talk about Bina in front of him? Unless, of course, they had no idea that he had designs on her.

But their explanation still didn't feel right, as if something was being kept from me.

As soon as Jeevan pulled up in the club car park, we were mobbed by young boys dressed in raggedy sweaters, darned in many places, and old plimsolls. Their eyes, bright and hopeful, searched out Nana.

"Me, me, me, sahib!"

Nani gently pushed her way through. "You *know* I have my regular caddy. Where is he?"

"Sick, memsahib, sick. Take me!"

"No me!"

"Stop it!" Nani spoke in mock exasperation. "Who hasn't worked today?" All the boys yelled: Me! Me! Me!

Nani pointed to a boy of about twelve with a navy balaclava pulled over his head, so only his eyes and little brown nose were visible. He saluted smartly and gleefully grabbed the cart with her golf set.

Nana's caddy was a skinny, older man who greeted him like a friend. He, too, saluted and set off in the direction of the course, pulling Nana's trolley behind him, while we three went to the clubhouse, a white mock-Tudor building. Inside the deep verandah people wearing golfer's gear were drinking tea and chatting.

Princess Vidya was talking animatedly to Nana's partner, who was introduced as the retired police commissioner, Mr Chowdhry. She stubbed out a cigar and shouted at the top of her voice, "Koshy! Come here – I must tell you the funniest thing I've heard in ages! You know that nincompoop Mrs Singh has told my laundryman that because her son in England has sent a set of linen from Harrods, the poor dhobi has to hand wash sheets and pillowcases in Genteel soap!"

Nani smiled, although I noticed a certain look passed between the former police commissioner and Nana. It was just like the looks our gang used to exchange. I suddenly missed Grania and Elizabeth, and realized I hadn't been been homesick for days.

The game began with the men marching ahead, in that peculiar stiff-kneed way of old soldiers. I heard snatches of conversation about how terrible the government was and how some judge had taken a huge bribe and bought a vintage car with the money. They slapped one another on the back, laughed noisily like schoolboys.

They hit the ball with fierce concentration and said, "Well done, sir!" when it sailed up. When it went into the bushes they said, "Oh, bad luck, sir!"

Wherever it landed – on the fairway or in the rough – a caddy would stand guard until the hitter of the ball arrived. Then the caddy suggested a suitable implement to hit it again: a wood for distance, an iron for accuracy.

"What do you bet?"

"The usual, old boy! Five chips on each win?"

Meanwhile Princess Vidya had tucked me under her wing and was busy giving instructions on the finer points of the game. She was Nana's regular partner, and Nani was the commissioner's. The princess, in her yellow cord trousers, green sweater and red baseball cap kept up a running commentary. "We're known as the Four Musketeers. Look at that foursome there trying to eavesdrop on my witticisms. How dare they!" She shook her iron at the players on a parallel hole. I saw them rocking with laughter. My skin crawled with embarrassment and I turned to Nani, but she was obviously immune to her friend's antics and just winked very slightly to show she understood my reaction.

Princess Vidya followed Nani's every move as she swung her slim hips to hit a graceful long drive. The little white ball climbed up and up into a perfect arc before dropping down a long way off.

"Good shot, I say," her opponent grudgingly conceded. It was her turn to hit so the princess planted her small feet firmly on the turf and waggled her club; I heard her muttering, "Watch this, snake hips – I'm going to win this shot!"

By now I had picked up that the fewer shots it took to put the ball into a hole, the higher you scored. The better you were as a player, the lower your handicap. Nana's was twelve and Nani's was eighteen. You could go on improving your handicap, which meant that you always had something to aim for, but improving it by just one point might take half a lifetime.

The princess spent a long time waggling her club before swivelling on her left foot and swinging back a hundred and eighty degrees to thwack the ball, but she missed.

"Bloody hell!" she spat out like it was the biggest disaster. I knew she was trying to impress me. On the next try she sliced the ball on top and it rolled pathetically into a bush about five yards away to the left.

"Ow, ow," came an agonized cry. The club had been flung aside and Princess Vidya was collapsed on the course, legs spread wide, like a small child, and her face twisted in a grimace. "Oh, oh, my shoulder!" she yelled. "I've twisted something. I can't play any more."

"Oh, what a shame," Nani said. "Go on, Sarla, go with Aunty Vidya to the clubhouse. The ayah in the ladies' room will massage your leg and make it better, Vidya. We'll have tea together when we've finished."

I wasn't clear how they could play without their fourth musketeer.

Princess Vidya almost pouted. "It's not my leg, it's my shoulder, silly!"

"Go on, darling, take care of her. Another two holes and we'll join you for tea and buttered toast."

After first lighting a cigar, the princess leaned on me and hobbled to the ladies' room.

"I thought it was your shoulder," I couldn't help saying.

"Yes, yes, it is; referred pain," she said enigmatically and took a puff of her foul cigar.

Her tantrums continued as the ayah, a wizened

old lady at least twenty years her senior, vigorously kneaded her shoulder. The patient's groans grew louder and her shrewd eyes focused on me.

"You know who she is? My old nanny! Her father was Daddy's chauffeur."

The old lady, wearing a beige cardigan buttoned up to her scrawny neck, smiled fondly, as though Vidya were still her little darling. The princess couldn't stop showing off. She reminded me of a child who always had to push people to their limit.

"I wasn't very nice to you, was I, when I was young?"

Ayah smiled delightedly as the princess tweaked her wrinkled cheek. "All the waiters and staff are descendants of my father's lackeys," she added in an offhand way.

I wasn't impressed, and it probably showed.

"At one time we had two hundred servants." She took a luxurious puff, even though a no smoking sign was staring her in the face. It made me cough.

She let out a regretful sigh. "That's how we royals lived – lavishly, no expenses spared! Rolls Royces, gun salutes. Do you know, if my grandfather wanted to execute a thief he'd just order a hanging – nothing like a trial or anything!"

I suppose she thought my eyes would widen, but I stayed cool. I'd heard of maharajahs, tiger shoots, harems, diamonds as big as pigeon eggs and it was all mixed up in my mind like the *Arabian Nights*, though I wasn't going to give her the pleasure of showing any interest.

The princess held out her hand for the poor ayah to haul her up. "I know what, Sarla, my little *firangi* – come for dinner tomorrow and I'll tell you all about my family and show you our treasures. History: you'll learn a lot of history! We were such a colourful lot! I'm not stopping for tea – I need a long soak. Tell Koshy I went home. But I'll send the car for you tomorrow at six thirty sharp."

"Thank you, Aunty Vidya, but I have an arrangement with Bina tomorrow evening," I lied. "Sorry, but I can come only if she's invited as well."

The princess's jaw dropped. I could hear her thinking, the cheek of the brat! She knew what I was up to, challenging her snobby ideas about who was worthy to be invited to The Retreat. She gave me a long, hard look, which was a bit scary, then suddenly she burst out laughing – a great wheezy guffaw. The ayah joined in like a court jester, even though she had no idea what the joke was about.

"I knew it!" she said congratulating herself. "A chip off the old block. Just like your mother, Rita. Yes, why not? We should look after these people, give them a chance to better themselves – so bring Bina with you."

She waddled off with a cheery wave and I collapsed on a stool, not sure if I was going to laugh or cry. *These people.* It was the first time I'd ever met anyone who thought she was so superior to others. But in spite of myself I couldn't help being intrigued. It would be interesting to see her palace, even if she was the crassest person I'd ever encountered; and of course the gorgeous Sidhartha would be there too.

Grown-ups think they're invincible. I suppose it comes with the whole package of power, authority, being old and wise and all that stuff. Even the nicest grown-ups think they can pretend and get away with it. It's normal for kids to challenge them – they try and discourage it but we do it anyway. I suppose that's what most rows are about.

I saw right through Nana when he asked me, "What do you think of our dear princess?" There were no obvious clues, but I smelled a mean motive, in spite of – or maybe because of – his casual tone. He lowered his paper to see how I would react to his question.

In fact, Nani betrayed him. "Now, *meri jaan*, don't be nasty. She has a good heart, even though her family life was far from happy. First, that awful old father, the maharajah, then her husband Bunty killed so young, no children, nobody to look after her in her old age…"

"I can forgive anyone anything, except when they cheat at games. That Vidya is the biggest cheat of all."

"And the biggest snob, not to mention bully," I added.

"But you got her to invite Bina, which shows she has another side to her," Nani said, sticking up for her friend.

Nana sniffed and went back to *The Times of India*.

"Anyway, you'll have a very interesting evening. I'll lend you my lovely pashmina shawl to go with your new salwar kameez."

Jeevan the Creep was lurking around the Ambassador, giving it a desultory rub. As Bina came out his eyes slid after her. The tune he was humming sounded cheeky and flirtatious to me. Was I right guessing he had a thing for her?

She was very twitchy, fiddling in a neurotic kind of way as we hung around waiting for the chauffeur to pick us up in the Bentley: she played with her hair, examined her nails, twisted her hanky, shuffled her feet, sniffed, scratched her chin restlessly. I found her more and more of a puzzle. How was I going to ever read someone so ... so *mysterious*? What was she thinking about? What went on underneath her placid expression?

As we sailed away in the car, she sat tense and expressionless, playing with her silly hanky. But her new green silk outfit patterned with yellow roses looked good. I sneaked a glance at her profile and had to admit that she was much more attractive than me – much thinner and prettier. Her long thick hair was up in a simple bun, she had on dangly earrings made of some dark red stone that caught the light in a subtle way, there was a suspicion of lipstick and she'd changed her plimsolls for kitten heels. Of course! Why hadn't I guessed? She was trying to look her best for Sidhartha. For certain, now I didn't stand a chance in that direction.

We didn't talk (although that would have been nice) just enjoyed the gloriously soft leather seats, but when we turned a corner and the summer palace came into view, a gasp of wonder, a sound like *"Pheoof!"* emerged from the Sphinx. It was a pretty amazing sight.

The Retreat resembled a Scottish castle. It was built of huge brown stones (granite?) with battlements and windows with tiny panes, but minus the drawbridge. Like a film set, The Retreat looked almost unreal against a technicolour sky and dramatic black clouds. We swept up a crunchy drive, and were ceremoniously escorted by the chauffeur to the massive wooden door studded with nails and iron bars. He tugged a bell-rope and a butler let us in. We waited in the dim hall, leered at by snarling tigers, sad-looking deer and stuffed birds in glass cases.

The sun had set behind the mountains and it felt almost spooky in there, when Sidhartha appeared out of nowhere, even more handsome than I'd remembered. I could feel Bina tensing up next to me, looking stern and stiff and unsmiling, which only confirmed what I'd guessed.

"Come on into the sitting room and have a drink. *Nimboo pani*, Fanta? Aunt is having a shower – she'll be along in a minute. Now you are Sarla and this is Bina? Have I got your names the right way round?" He spoke in a formal, polite and rather courtly way and moved with confidence and a kind of controlled energy.

He led the way to an enormous, dark space crammed with furniture, pictures, clocks and silver. Why did it look vaguely familiar? Of course, it was a stately home, like Osborne House, which used to be Queen Victoria's summer palace. We'd gone there on a school trip.

The butler drew the heavy dark red brocade curtains and switched on the lights. A great sparkling chandelier illuminated love seats — those strange S-shaped sofas for Victorian flirts — other pieces of carved furniture, tables with corkscrew legs, a grand piano and lots of silver ornaments arranged in groups on every available surface. China figurines, such as ballerinas and shepherdesses, added to the clutter and the pictures were typically Victorian — stags drinking from streams and white-capped Swiss mountains.

As I soaked it all up my eyes lit on an enormous gilt-framed portrait hanging over the fireplace. A flame-haired European woman in a blue ball-gown, posing like a forties film star, loomed over us. Who on earth was she, and why did she have pride of place in the room?

We were offered nuts and canapés and we chit-chatted about my impressions of Daroga. Soon after, Princess Vidya made a dramatic entrance. She paused in the doorway in her evening clothes — much like her day wear: lurid trousers and a clashing sweatshirt, but no baseball-cap — and greeted us in her normal booming fashion. "Is he looking after you?" Then she bellowed, "Ram Singh!" and when the subdued-looking butler hurried in, "My usual, and hurry up, you lazy sod! Where have you been all this time?"

She stretched out her hand for her glass of whisky, stirred it with a silver cocktail stick and took a thirsty swallow. "That's better."

Probably an alcoholic, I thought, notching up another black mark against her.

"Well, well. Nice to see you both." She stared, not at all curiously or from genuine interest, but as if we were specimens in a lab. Settling herself comfortably into an overstuffed sofa like a buddha, she finally had her audience.

"Where shall I start?"

Bina was playing with her glass. Sidhartha's grey eyes were fixed on the carpet. Was he embarrassed by the princess or immune to her whims? Since neither he nor Bina were about to start a scintillating conversation, I broke the silence.

"Who is the lady in the portrait?"

Nine

&

BINA

My breathing was so shallow that I was afraid I might faint. The room and everyone in it looked hazy, but I could hardly look up. It was the first time it had happened to me, but it couldn't be anything else. I had fallen in love! Every time he looked at me, every time he said something I felt my arms and legs go weak. My cheeks were hot, on fire. My whole body felt clumsy and self-conscious as though everyone's attention was on me, seeing right through me.

I'd seen him before, had had a harmless crush on him; in my dreams he was the most handsome man I'd ever set eyes on, but I'd never been in the same room with him. I'd never talked to him.

He was more perfect than I'd imagined – so polite and gentle. I liked the sound of his voice and the way he moved. I liked the way he held his drink – he had beautiful hands! I noticed he didn't show irritation towards his aunt, though she was enough to try anyone's patience. So I was in a complete daze when Princess Vidya stood up and said loudly, "A toast! A toast to Her Royal Highness, the late Maharani Rajeshwari Sundari, Queen Mirela, my dearest mother, who passed away at the tender age of twenty-four. She was a *shaheed*, a martyr, to love."

Sarla and Sidhartha got up and also raised their glasses, so I copied them.

"The late maharani!" Sidhartha took a sip of Pepsi, so I also drank a bit of Fanta. What was this strange ritual these grand people did in honour of the dead?

"That, my dear Sarla, is who you are looking at. The lady in the evening gown is my mother, painted here by the famous Russian painter Nicholas Roerich. Mother came from Romania and she died, *died*, giving birth to me. It had a terrible effect on my life." Her face crumpled, her lip wobbled. The princess suddenly looked like a baby about to start wailing for its milk. She held out her glass to be refilled and motioned to us to sit down.

"You see where he gets his eyes from," she pointed at Sidhartha.

"Romania?" Sarla exclaimed. "How did she come to Daroga?"

I didn't even know where Romania was. I would look it up in the atlas when I got home.

The princess cleared her throat. "My mother was a circus artist – the greatest trapeze artiste in Europe. Her circus used to take the land route to India travelling from Vienna, across Eastern Europe, crossing the Bosphorus into Turkey, Iran, Afghanistan, over the Himalayas through the Khyber Pass into India. It took a year to travel overland, coming slowly south with their lions and tigers, their dancing bears, their prancing horses trained in Vienna, their acrobats and magicians and their star: Mirela, the trapeze artiste!

"One day they arrived in our state, where of course my father was maharajah. He already had two wives but when he saw Mirela it was love at first sight."

My heart thumped: love at first sight! I knew what that felt like. But how could it be that the princess's mother had been in a circus? When the circus had been to Daroga the people in it looked like gipsies: dirty and shabby, the children with runny noses and the women with bold made-up eyes and red lipstick. If her mother was one of them, then Princess Vidya wasn't the high and mighty person she seemed. Half of her must be even lower in caste than me!

From the corner of my eye I noticed someone shuffling in the doorway. Ram Singh, her servant, was trying to say something. After some minutes he came timidly up to her, bowed and whispered that dinner was served. My grandfather would never have been afraid like that of Uncleji, but this poor man was like a scared rabbit, rightly so because Princess Vidya nearly bit off his head. She roared, "Can't you see I'm talking?"

"Don't worry, Ram Singh, we're on our way. Come on, Aunt, the food will get cold. Our guests must be hungry and we can hear your story at the table."

Sidhartha held out his hand to help her. I got the feeling that he was a kind of shield against Princess Vidya's outbursts. The servants must love him, and my heart warmed to him. He briefly touched Ram Singh's shoulder and once we had been shown to our chairs he pulled out his aunt's first and then mine to help us sit down.

I often ate with Koshy Aunty and Uncleji, but not like this. This table was laid with sparkling silver, porcelain and crystal. There were two sets of cutlery for each of us, but the princess ate with her hands. The servants offered us dish after dish: koftas, curried venison, chicken, and all kinds of vegetables. There were pooris and tandoori roti and many pickles and chutneys. I love pickles, but we only have the simple ones like lemon and mango at home. I tried the stuffed chilli pickle, the cauliflower and turnip, sweet and sour pork, tomato and ginger and so many others that made my mouth water, in little silver dishes with matching spoons.

I was amazed by the princess's appetite – she got through about five pooris and three helpings each of the main dishes. No wonder she had a weight problem! Her whisky glass stayed close to her. She drained it and looked at me.

"Now where was I? Ah yes, the circus that came winding down our mountain roads, with trumpets and drums and banners announcing the show; Signor Paolo the ringmaster cracking his whip – so fine in his breeches and polished riding boots – and then my dear mother: riding sidesaddle on a pure white horse, in a silver lamé outfit, a rifle across her knee. Papa fell for her there and then. He was watching from the verandah of the shopping arcade in town, and he proposed the next day. His first gift to her was a ring of white gold set with the famous Anarkali diamond."

The princess was so caught up in her story she seemed hypnotized; she certainly had us all under her spell. Even Sidhartha, who had heard it many times before, was listening attentively.

"But there was a complication … Mother was married: to Signor Paolo."

Sarla's hand stopped halfway to her mouth. "What happened? What did your father do?"

Loud laugh. "Challenged the signor to a duel! Papa was an ace Olympic fencer and he won. Mind you, he did slice off the ringmaster's ear." She guffawed.

Only Sarla would have dared say, "Uggh!"

"But I think all's fair in love and war, don't you? Dearest Mama became his third wife and she first bore him a son – Dinkoo's father, my brother, who is a nutter, isn't he, Sid? A year later she died giving birth to me. She worshipped Papa. He gave her absolutely everything she could possibly want: status, a title, diamonds galore, trips to the south of France, a yacht in the Med, couture from Paris. Mama loved her horses too and bred some wonderful racehorses. After she died, Papa also died a little. For a long time he couldn't bear to look at me. My brother was his favourite and he spoiled him rotten. Not that it did him any good." Her face darkened.

Why, what had happened to her brother, Sidhartha's father? I would ask Koshy Aunty.

"Would you like to see a film of my mother doing her trapeze act? Dinks, you know where it is – go and fetch it from the safe in the library."

We were at the pudding stage and the princess had sunk into a reflective mood. I was just thinking, poor thing, she also never knew her mother, when she singled me out for attention, as though she had read my mind.

"You see, Bina, we have something in common after all. What is the news of your poor mother? I hear that Antonia is very faithful and writes regularly, but does she ever get a reply?"

At least she didn't shout it out. She had lowered her voice, but Sarla heard of course. It startled her and there was a sudden crash as her elbow caught her glass and water spilled all the way down the table. The servants came to mop it up, and then Sidhartha returned with the reel of film. I was grateful that the princess didn't carry on questioning me – thank God – Sidhartha hadn't heard anything. I resigned myself for a grilling by Sarla on the way back home.

We could hardly see anything in the old fuzzy film, just some movement of a figure swinging from her knees. The projector was also ancient, whirring like a mechanical insect behind us. It was time to go so we said our thank yous. Sidhartha made a vague offer about talking some more to me about medical college. He said I should call him. As if!

As soon as we were on our way Sarla demanded,

like I knew she would, "What was all that about your mother?"

"Sshh," I indicated the chauffeur in front.

She wouldn't give up. She whispered, "Come on, Bina. You have to tell me something more about yourself. Remember, I'm here for another six weeks. That's a long time to play dumb. Anyway, you promised you'd explain and you've been avoiding me since that evening. What's the real story? I thought your mother died in a car crash."

"Not now." I wouldn't be able to hold out much longer; she had won, so I gave in. I'd been told not to say anything about my parents, but there was no escaping her prying.

"I'll tell you, but somewhere safe, where no one can hear us. Come over tomorrow at teatime and I'll explain."

I shut my eyes. Enough was enough. Enough of the princess, who pretended to be more blue-blooded than she really was, enough of Sarla with her endless curiosity. I crawled into my shell and refused to say another word. It had been an exhausting evening and I was drained.

Ten

🦌

SARLA

My first two weeks had just flown, though I felt I'd been there for ages. I'd strolled into Daroga bazaar, had new clothes made, taken Carmen for walks by myself, been to the golf club, and got used to a completely different way of life: delicious food, everything orderly, spick and span, done regularly and on time; my grandparents, present and available; Hira, Lila and so many people to chat with; old photo albums to look at and so much to think about, especially the unfathomable Bina.

I'd also thought about Sidhartha, and wondered if he had a girlfriend in Chandigarh. I wondered why Princess Fatty had called his dad a nutter. Was he a real loony, or just eccentric? And Fatty's mother, the trapeze queen: did she become a Hindu when she married the maharajah? Was she burnt on a funeral pyre when she died, or did she remain whatever Romanians were, and was she buried in the old churchyard? I'd taken a quick look on one of my walks. It was grossly overcrowded with gravestones of dead English people, all tipping over, pitted, mossy, and really creepy.

As I'd tiptoed round I'd nearly had a heart attack when I'd come upon a bundle of rags stretched out on a slab. It was an old, brown Tibetan woman. Her hair was all matted, her wrinkles scored deeply into her face. She'd raised her head and opened her black mouth wide, but I had hurried back through the broken gate before she could say anything. Another time I'd seen a young woman, also matted and filthy-looking, wandering around aimlessly clapping her hands, laughing. She was lost in her own world.

The following day – Saturday – Bina had morning school. After she'd seen to her schoolwork we set off for her house and the meeting for which I'd been waiting on tenterhooks. Hira and Lila hovered anxiously giving her instructions: "Open the new packet of biscuits and, here, take these samosas for your tea! Don't forget to put a cloth on the table!"

Hira beamed, "Very good you go to our house with Bina, making friends, talking English. I come and fetch you before dark. *Tata*, Baby!"

Their home was less than half a mile away, in a small hamlet clustered behind Stoneleigh. Bina strode in a purposeful way, surefooted as a goat. We went across a small meadow, then down a gully. Near their house was a small white temple and I saw a priest with a shaven head staring at us as we passed.

Bina unlocked a heavy padlock and we stepped straight into the living room. It had no windows, but rays of afternoon sun slid down the room from high skylights. There was a divan, some wooden chairs and a low table.

She explained, "This is where I sleep." We walked through another door leading to a cloister-like verandah that went all round the small house with a brick-paved courtyard in the middle. A kitchen, a bathroom and one other room led off and behind the kitchen there was a tin-roofed cowshed.

"Come and say hello to my Gulabi," Bina said, switching on a radio in the kitchen. The sound of violins and a woman singing in a teasing high voice brought a festive air to the chilly house. Gulabi mooed in her shed. She was chewing away and was a well-fed creature, unlike the skeleton we'd met in the bazaar. Bina threw down some straw and filled the feeding trough. Bina murmured something loving to her cow as we left the shed and went to rinse her hands under the kitchen tap.

"Now, do you want to see how I make pakoras?" She grabbed a handful of spinach from a plastic basket. I made polite noises, though I was impatient for her to tell me her story. After fifteen minutes when nothing significant had been said, I suspected that she was stalling. If we didn't get on with it, Hira would appear and I'd have to go back to Stoneleigh without finding out anything.

"Forget all this hostess stuff, Bina. You promised to talk to me – let's not waste more time. I want to know why you were crying, and please tell me the truth about your mother. I thought she was dead, but now I hear she's alive and getting letters from Piloo's friend Antonia! So what is really going on?"

Bina didn't answer but carried on making tea in a pot, laying out biscuits and samosas on plates; only when the table in the front room had been set to her liking did she draw up a chair and gesture for me to sit. She fingered the gold locket round her neck while she looked at me, sizing me up, hesitating, before dropping down on her knees and dragging out a steel trunk under the divan-bed. There were two brass locks, one on each side. She unlocked them, raised the lid and started to take out piles of embroidered linen: sheets and pillowcases, antimacassars and tablecloths, all beautifully worked in coloured threads. She laid them neatly on the divan and from the bottom of the trunk extracted a large brown manila envelope.

She held it out saying, "Go on then. This will tell you everything you want to know."

I peered inside the bulging envelope. It was stuffed with newspaper articles, letters and documents. I handed it back to her with a shrug; where was I supposed to begin?

She shook out the papers, arranging them in an order only known to her. Then she selected a black and white photograph. It was so badly creased that white cracks showed through, but I made out the figure of a woman dressed in trousers, in a kind of military uniform with a bullet-studded belt and a rifle in her right hand.

"Who's this?" I asked, though I thought I knew.

"This is my mother: Shobharani Devi."

"Is she a bank robber? Why is she dressed like this? What's she doing with a gun?"

"She has another name – Bandit Queen of the Hills. She was not an ordinary robber; she helped the poor and they made her into their own goddess. You see, devi means goddess," she said with a touch of pride. "They are waiting for her to come back to them."

I hadn't expected anything like this. I was

completely dumbstruck. I stared harder at the photo trying to make sense of it. A robber who was a goddess? Bina's mother? How crazy was that? But I knew that Bina was telling the truth. She'd gone pale and very still. This truth was stranger than any story I could have made up.

The woman in the picture had Bina's small nose and high forehead. Her eyes were deep-set, staring at the camera in a way that reminded me of Bina. She looked familiar, but I couldn't think why. Who else did she remind me of? Her long black hair curled below her shoulders, framing a face that was angry and bitter and beautiful at the same time. A hundred questions were forming in my mind, but before I could ask any, Bina thrust a yellowed newspaper cutting in my hand. While I read she perched on the edge of the divan, leaning forward to pour two cups of tea.

A photo of Shobharani in handcuffs, her head hanging limp like a chicken, headed the article.

TIGRESS IS TRAPPED AFTER FIERCE ENCOUNTER

After years of being chased through jungles and mountains, the notorious woman dacoit, Shobharani, was cornered in a wild and lonely part of the Himalayan foothills. Many of the gang – led by her and Beharilal, the ex-policeman – were killed by Special Branch Force at a bloody shoot-out in Ghata Fort, to the south-east of the state. Her lover Beharilal died later in hospital.

Shobharani's gang was surrounded in the early hours following a tip-off.

After a fierce gun battle between the police and the gang – known locally as "Companions of the Goddess" – the Bandit Queen was taken in handcuffs to Ambala Central Jail, where she will be held until her trial later this month.

It was a humiliating end for the woman who gave up everything to elope with Beharilal. For over fourteen years she has lived a life of dangerous risk-taking, adventure and drama. Now the adventure is over and she will be tried for dozens of criminal offences, including murder, armed robbery and extortion.

A life sentence is expected for the woman who terrorized wealthy landowners and farmers to share her loot with the poor and downtrodden of the countryside.

Her case has stimulated much debate among human rights organizations and feminists, who have argued that Shobharani is a victim of male oppression and systemic gender imbalance.

When I finished reading, Bina passed over another cutting. This one far more recent:

MORE SINNED AGAINST THAN SINNING?

Exclusive interview with the Bandit Queen of the Hills,
by our own correspondent

I was allowed to meet the legendary Shobharani in
the prison interview room, a bleak, windowless place.
I had just half an hour to question this extraordinary
woman who lived for years in conditions that would
make many men recoil. In the heat of summer and the
freezing conditions of winter this lifer lived in the open
with her twenty male companions, one of whom was
the love of her life, Beharilal, the policeman turned
armed robber.

Although well past forty she is still a beauty. She
is small-boned, lean and tanned, with long hair and
observant eyes. She speaks with authority, which she
earned as the leader of men. There is stinging venom
when she demands, "What did life ever offer me? I was
married when I was a child, beaten black and blue by
my husband and mother-in-law; and for what? Because
I didn't bring a big dowry – no fridge, scooter, Benares
saris – so I was as worthless as the dirt under their
shoes! The day I tried to defend myself I became a
criminal in their eyes and the eyes of the law."

I ask about her background, but she would not
respond to any questions about her parentage. All I
can gather is that her father was in the army and both
parents are dead. Her in-laws are so terrified of

reprisals that they have changed their name and left the state. Rumour has it that she had a daughter from her marriage but no one has been able to verify this.

Shobharani was the mistress of disguise. Members of her gang would dress as *hijras* (transvestites) and mingle with wedding parties. Before the festivities had ended the wedding guests had been relieved of jewellery and cash and the *hijras* had taken off for their hideout. The money was often distributed to the poor: landless labourers and stone-breakers. Acts like these endeared the Bandit Queen to locals, who revered her as their saviour and goddess.

Latterly Shobharani started to harass local government institutions in conducting terrorist acts aimed at bringing about a separate hill state. She was reputed to be always on the side of defenceless women and famous for championing lower caste victims of society.

When I tell her that many international organizations are pleading for leniency and that academics in universities are keen to write books about her and others in her plight, she smiles sceptically. It seems that she lost faith in established society and values long ago.

Suddenly her mood changes and she starts to shout and pound her fists against the wall. She knocks her head against the hard surface until she is restrained, rather roughly. Now I can see a different face: haunted and forlorn; a face devoid of hope; the face of someone who fights the demons within during every hour of her existence.

She is led away by the warders, a sad, mentally ill woman who has given up on life after experiences that would have scorched anyone. The wonder is that she survived so long.

I could hardly take it in. All of a sudden the small safe world of Daroga, my grandparents, my mother, myself was transformed into a space full of unfamiliar danger and menace. Without wanting to, I'd travelled on a magic carpet and come to a dark country full of demons and unimaginable horrors. I shivered. How did Bina live with this knowledge? How had she survived? No wonder she was unlike anyone I'd ever met, and no wonder I hadn't understood her.

Bina was hunched up on her divan-bed, knees drawn up, a tear sliding down her cheek. Of course – it dawned on me that she had no way of guessing how I would take these revelations. For all she knew I was so horrified that I'd draw back and not want to speak to her any more. I was overcome with pity and terrible sadness for her.

Not at all sure how she would react, I put my hand on her knee. "I'm so sorry." For a minute I was ashamed that I'd more or less bullied her into sharing her painful story with me. I also started to understand why she couldn't be open about herself; I certainly wouldn't have liked to broadcast about Rita to the world if she were locked away. " It must have been awful for you. Tell me more."

So she told me, getting really angry one minute, grinding her teeth and beating the bed with her fist, crying the next minute as she poured out the story of her growing up.

"Can you imagine keeping a secret like this? It was hammered into me that no one should know. I've always felt so alone. And then my grandfather keeps threatening to marry me off, to get me out of the way. That is not the life I want! Sometimes I think I should run away, but then how will I ever get to university and qualify as a doctor? When I'm really down I feel it's such an impossible dream it will never happen."

"Don't say that! You have to be strong and it will happen! Bina, my mum will help you. She's been a single parent and worked ever so hard to get to the top. And Nana and Nani will never let you down. You know they won't."

I had my arms round Bina when the front door suddenly opened and Hira walked in.

It took a few seconds for me to realize that he wasn't pleased with the scene in front of him. He looked at the scattered papers, the open trunk and Bina weeping on the divan. And as I saw his face become grimmer and his whole body tense up, I was afraid. My heart jumped as I saw him stride over to Bina, his hand raised and ready to strike.

"Stop it! How dare you hit her!"

He ignored me, but he did lower his hand. I didn't understand what he said to her because he spoke in Hindi, but whatever it was she cowered and burst into sobs.

I'd had no idea that Hira could be so mean to his own granddaughter. I'd only seen him trying to please me, saying Baby this and Baby that. Wait till Nani and Nana heard about this! For the first time in my life I was afraid of the physical strength of a man. He could have snapped Bina in two if he'd wanted.

"Let's go, Bina," I shouted. "I've had enough of this. Let's get out of here, back to Nana and Nani."

I took her hand and dragged her outside. We ran all the way back in the rain. It was nearly dark and when we reached the back gate we were both drenched. Jeevan was waiting just inside the gate. He opened a big black umbrella and held it over Bina. I had run on ahead so I couldn't hear what he said to her, but as I looked back to see if she was following I saw her give him a sharp push. She ran towards the verandah and he angrily shook his finger at her. It was too much – two nasty, angry men in one afternoon.

"Let's go and dry out in my room." I dragged Bina inside before anyone could see how upset she was. There were lots more questions to be answered and the story was far from complete.

Eleven

Four young Liberation Front men had volunteered to journey to the other side of the country. Somehow there was enough money in the kitty to buy the train fares to Patna, in the east of India. From there they would catch a bus to Purulia and take delivery of the long-awaited guns. The airdrop of arms was expected on a day that hadn't been specified exactly, but that it would be inside the last week in July was definitely confirmed. The commander-in-chief of the Liberation Front came to the station at Ambala to see them off. Being on the Special Branch wanted list, he had disguised himself with wire-rimmed glasses and grown a beard. The Liberation boys looked like a carefree group of students on a jolly summer holiday, armed with water bottles, a transistor radio and cloth bags on their shoulders.

The C-in-C could have been their professor – in fact he was known as "Prof". He slipped the leader a piece of paper with a vehicle registration and phone number written on it. "That's the goods truck; cargo: sugarcane. Travel back to Chandigarh in this truck and no other. The driver will be waiting to hear from you by phone, and you can arrange a pick-up point between you. Remember, do not take any other form of transport back home. You can hide the bomb-making equipment and firearms under the cane and the truck driver has enough money to bribe nosy policemen. Good luck!" He gave the young man a friendly shove.

Six days later they were in Purulia, a mean little village inhabited by local tribespeople who smoked a kind of grass that kept them on a permanent high. They kept small black pigs that ran here and there, inside and outside their mud and grass huts. The villagers had very little Hindi, but from the headman's gestures the boys gathered that they were not allowed to sleep in the village compound, but must strike camp some way off. The headman showed them how to weave camouflage capes and caps from leaves. "Police!" he said fiercely, opening wide his red eyes.

So they waited, foraging for food in the dense forest, sometimes getting a meal of thin porridge with lentils from the villagers. They were in a new and unfamiliar environment – a dense rainforest, different from the tall pines and cool air of the mountains – so they didn't get bored waiting. During the day they amused themselves watching exotic birds and animals. At night they kept a lookout on the edge of a clearing in the jungle, where the parachutes – hopefully – would drop from the sky into their hands. The night was full of sounds: the yelping of hyenas, chatter of monkeys, birds that called with whooping cries.

On the night of the full moon, towards the end of their second week, they heard a strange groaning noise a long way off, which became louder and louder. It could have been a wild elephant on heat, but they knew it must be the airplane.

It was an ancient and noisy craft and it circled the clearing a few times before moving away. When it returned a little later there was a second plane that followed, a much faster aircraft. Both were flying quite low. The boys could just make out the shapes in the moonlight, and that the second plane was a jet. Both planes moved away and then there was silence.

"What happened?" they were asking each other, when suddenly a group of villagers came crashing through the jungle waving their spears. "Go, go! Police are coming!"

They were pushed out of their camp and made to run until they came to a river bank. They got into a leaky rowing boat and were rowed down river by a villager. They disembarked close to a track. The boatman waved his oar. Away, away, go back home. The mission was over, with nothing to show for it. Something had gone terribly wrong.

Later they found out that the second plane had been an Indian Air Force jet that had forced down the first craft carrying their guns and supplies. The national papers and news were full of the conspiracy to smuggle arms into the territory. The

145

pilot and two passengers had been arrested and the deadly cargo impounded. The three men were all foreigners – a Russian and two Frenchmen – who were locked up in jail in Patna waiting for an enquiry into the biggest arms-smuggling operation ever seen in India.

It was a huge consignment, bought and paid for by some foreign agency or government working against the interest of India, Nepal and even Myanmar. The arms were meant for rebels and insurgents to overthrow established governments, but nothing could be proved. Myanmar and Nepal were virtual dictatorships, but India was a democracy. The sense of outrage went on for weeks and months in the press and parliament.

The Liberation Front boys met the sugarcane truck and got back to the Daroga hills. No arms, no supplies and therefore no forward plan. The army was after them, their C-in-C was lying low. Nothing had worked out as it should have done. They were desperately short of money, and because nothing could move forward without money, something else would have to be done.

Twelve

SARLA

I got to the point. "What is going on between you and that slimy driver?"

Bina was drying her hair with my towel. Hira hadn't returned from his house to Stoneleigh, my grandparents were out, so there was a window of opportunity to get the truth out of her.

"I know he likes you – I caught him staring at you the other day, and he's always singing under his breath when you go anywhere near him. And why was he getting mad at you just now?"

She twisted a turban round her head. Her eyes looked huge. "He wants to marry me. He says he'll tell the whole town about my mother if I don't agree. The night you found me crying, he was bullying me and I was terrified. I didn't know what to do."

"So that's what's been going on! And *so*?"

"Don't be stupid, Sarla! *Think* for a minute. If they know at school, I'll have to leave. Then my grandfather will force me to marry some idiot and I'll never become a doctor and get out of this awful little town, will I?"

"What a fatalist. Come on, there has to be a way to stop that pathetic little worm. What I don't get is why you're such a victim! What is it about you, Bina? Why haven't you told Antonia – won't she help you?"

"Sarla," she said patiently, "you don't understand how things work here. OK, what do you think Antonia will do? She'll come straight to Aunty Koshy; Jeevan will get sacked; Grandfather will find out the reason behind his sacking (meanwhile of course Jeevan will have spread the scandal all over town); some girl's parents will complain to Mother Superior; I'll have to leave school; Grandfather will get me married off. Point made."

"It's clear we have to get another person to help us." I couldn't think whom, so I smiled, trying to make her lighten up. "This is too hard, even for me."

She muttered, "It's not your problem but thanks for the offer." Then suddenly she cried, "My scarf, where is it? Where did I put it? Oh God, Sarla, my blue dupatta. Have you seen my dupatta? I had it just now. Wait, I must go and find it."

She ran off just as Nana and Nani came back from visiting their next-door neighbours. I poked my head into the sitting room and saw Hira waiting to talk to them, his face like thunder. He must have come in through the pantry door, without us hearing anything. Stoneleigh was a complex house. The sitting room was in the middle of the house, one side of which led to the dining room, kitchen and pantry. The other side went off into the bedrooms and Nana's study; the glazed verandah covered the whole front of the house.

Bina came back, closing my bedroom door behind her. She looked panic-stricken.

"My dupatta's gone: he's picked it up. Now he has another thing on me – he'll tell Grandfather that I was with him. He'll blackmail me for sure!"

Somehow I got her to calm down. "He won't do anything right away, so let's sleep on it. Trust me, I'm sure we'll find a way to deal with Jeevan!"

After breakfast next morning, Nana said, "Do you remember how we used to walk around the garden, you and I? Will you come with me? I have to see how old Bholuram is doing. I wanted him to put extra manure on the peas, but he may have forgotten – he's getting old and doddery like me."

He put on his shooting cap and picked up his

walking stick. He looked a bit tired because Hira and he had had a marathon session late into the night. Hira was nowhere to be seen that morning, and Lila and Nani had made breakfast between them. Because it was Sunday, Bina hadn't gone to school. She had come from her house and crept into Stoneleigh early. As usual she was busy doing her homework on the verandah. Carmen was resting her head on her foot.

I'd slept until five a.m. and then I'd dozed, thinking about what had happened the day before. Everything had changed. I felt quite unsettled knowing what I'd heard, but the result of being privy to Bina's secrets was that she and I had become friends.

My thoughts had wandered to princess Vidya as well, and Sidhartha. Not one of us four had had an ordinary upbringing. The Princess had grown up without love and attention. It seemed Sidhartha had a weird father. Bina had the strangest family of all; and I – who'd always thought I suffered from not having a proper family life – well, maybe I was the most normal of us all!

Bholuram the gardener was waving a black hosepipe, making arcs of small rainbows where it caught the morning sunshine. The vegetable patch was just as I remembered it: not a weed to be seen;

carrots, cabbages, peas, aubergines and lettuce, all in straight lines like soldiers.

"Bholuramji, did you notice it rained last night?" Nana asked in English for my benefit, then he said it jovially in Hindi. They talked about the manure, I suppose, and Nana did his rounds, lifting grey cabbage leaves to look for grubs underneath, poking and prodding. We wandered down to the edge of the garden, where there was a fantastic view of the hills opposite. Everything was green and clean in the morning air.

"Do some yogic breathing," Nana told me, demonstrating how to breathe quickly and deeply, sucking in my stomach. I felt very happy being there with him, being shown how to do something new.

Nana began, "I wanted to talk to you because Hira told me what happened yesterday. It's taken hours and hours to calm him down. You know he wants Bina to marry a weedy young man in Ambala? I have made it clear that Nani and I absolutely forbid it. Bina must finish her education and get a decent qualification, which we will continue to pay for."

He paused, distracted by something that Bholuram was doing.

"Not that one, the other one – prune the other one! Sorry," he went on. "It gives us a lot of satisfaction to think that she won't – God willing – go the way of her poor mother. But Hira can't see the long-term benefits: he's got a real kink about girls getting married young."

"Even when it was a disaster for Shobharani?"

"He thinks it wouldn't have happened if he'd been around. That's always been a big black mark against Lila, poor thing, as if she hasn't paid the price a hundred times over. The thing is, Sarla, we have to be very careful with Hira − very gentle and tactful. He had a hard time when he was a soldier and I have to look after him now; just as he looks after us."

Nana looked at me meaningfully. Becoming old meant being dependent. In England, ancients (as we called them) went into sheltered housing, like Elizabeth's granny, or if they were really old and ill, into care homes. In India they had the chance to stay put and have servants look after them.

I knew exactly what Nana was saying: if Hira and Lila were to leave, our lives would become impossible. I wondered if Rita and Piloo would ever give up their careers to come and live with their parents. It was hard to imagine Rita living in Daroga, fetching them cups of tea and playing Scrabble by the fire. My grandparents and Bina's grandparents, all of them, needed one another.

But I still couldn't understand why Hira and Lila

would rather Bina was unqualified; surely it would be better for her to be independent and earn her own money?

"They are terrified that she'll mix with boys at university, fall in love … you know what I mean. Escape, get out of their control."

"So it's better for everyone if she's some man's slave – just to be fed and taken care of?"

He smiled and lifted his eyebrows. "Also, if people find out who her mother is then Bina will suffer. We decided long ago that we didn't want her to see her mother again. I gather you know that Shobha is very unwell mentally and it would make Bina even more unhappy to be in contact with her."

Bholuram was standing by Nana, clearing his throat. He was holding something in his cupped hands. He offered me something. "*Dekho*, Baby."

Nestling in his palms was a tiny kitten, about three weeks old, its eyes barely open, mewing in a pitiful way. It was as small as a guinea pig, as small as Viktor in his animal heaven. It had the softest grey coat and white socks. "Nana, look at its tiny feet! We have to call it Socks."

"Probably from Antonia's menagerie up the hill. Somehow I don't think Nani will let you keep it."

She didn't, even when I pouted and flounced. "I haven't got the strength to take on another animal.

Carmen is quite enough. Take it back to Antonia after lunch – I know Bina has to arrange some extra dance lessons. She's back from Delhi and, as you know, she is Piloo's great friend."

But after lunch we had an unexpected visitor. Nosing up the drive came the princess's huge Bentley, and Sidhartha emerged from the driver's seat with a cheery wave.

"Just thought I'd drop in and offer my services: if you're going to the medical school you'll have lots of questions," he remarked casually to Bina. We were all sitting on the verandah, me with Socks on my lap. Nani gave him a shrewd look.

"Why don't you young people go and look up Antonia. We think she's lost a kitten."

Bina had gone all flustered and shy and I had no doubt that Sidhartha hadn't "just dropped in". It was obvious from the way he was looking at her (leaning towards her, so handsome in his sky-blue shirt ... oh, agony!) that he'd come to get a second sighting.

It suddenly came to me that this could be a brilliant opportunity. We might be able to enlist him in the campaign against Jeevan. I nearly shouted out *"Yesss!"*

Go on, go on, I was thinking, *fall for Bina, do it – now!*
Nani got up, shrugging on her beautifully un-

creased cardie. "We're off to play bridge with Vidya." I wondered if the princess cheated at cards as well as golf.

"I'll tell her that her nephew is busying himself with two beautiful young ladies."

"Oh, Nani," I cried. "You won't! That isn't fair, she'll have hysterics!" I could have bitten my tongue. But I don't think either Bina or Sidhartha paid any attention. They were busy talking shop about courses and professors and how much work there was – at least Sid was talking. Bina just gazed at him with dewy eyes. She looked as though she was lit up from inside.

I was sure Sid didn't have any shortage of admirers, so I wondered what he saw in Bina. Agreed, she was pretty. Two, she didn't giggle or behave in a silly way. Three, she had a kind of old-fashioned air: in romantic stories they'd call it dignity or poise. She didn't talk in clichés and she wasn't a spoilt rich girl. I suppose he saw enough of that kind; maybe, because she was unusual, from a different family background; maybe her shyness and reserve were a challenge to his male ego (I'd read my share of problem pages). Even more plausible, because *his* aunt would go barking mad at the prospect. Chemistry, whatever; you can't rationalize pheromones.

Bina, Sidhartha and I started off abreast, taking

up the whole width of the road. We turned left at the gate and started up a gentle incline. Apparently Antonia's was the last *pukka*, or proper, house before the next village.

It didn't take long before I was left straggling behind.

"I told you – why didn't you listen?" Bina called over her shoulder.

"I'm fine!" But my left foot kept turning over because my new platform sandals – those with the gold heels – wouldn't let me walk in a normal way.

Sidhartha came loping back. "Sarla, you'll twist your ankle. Just take them off and walk in bare feet."

Now I couldn't get off the right sandal, because the buckle was too stiff, so he made me sit down on the verge and worked it for me. He was grinning, but not unkindly. "Sorry: it's safer this way. Haven't brought elastic bandages or a first aid kit." He gave me an utterly sweet smile.

He would do. I felt he could be trusted. *If only they would fall in love!* He was too old for me anyway, so I nobly gave him up, didn't try and elbow into their conversation and decided to be on my best behaviour.

Ten minutes later we were standing under a rusting sign on the roadside. *Anjali Devi Dancing Academy*.

"So Antonia has an Indian name as well," I observed.

Bina nodded. "She wants to be as Indian as possible, but she looks completely English – you'll see."

Underneath the sign, wooden steps climbed up to a gate. On the small wicket gate was another sign, *The Nook*. A little wooden Ganesha was fixed on the trunk of a pine tree.

We entered a wild garden full of overgrown apple trees and then pandemonium broke out. Dogs started barking, cats yowling, birds screeching and a bloodcurdling human voice singing, running up and down a strange minor scale, shaking and gargling to the beat of drums and what must have been a harmonium.

"Ugghh!" I stuck my fingers in my ears.

"Stop it, Sarla, don't be rude," hissed Bina.

Three untidy dogs, black, brown and ginger, came running from the back and flung themselves at us, barking. The door opened and Antonia/Anjali stood there smiling at us. She was as untidy as her garden, brown hair escaping from a long plait, in salwar kameez with bells strapped to her ankles.

"Come in! How lovely to see you!"

Thirteen

❧

SARLA

Dark half-moons of sweat under her armpits, together with a whiff of powerful BO, gave the impression that Antonia was one of those arty females who thought shaving and deodorant a waste of time. She wiped beads of moisture on her forehead with her sleeve.

"Sorry, I'm all hot – been practising. What will you have? Tea? *Nimboo pani?* Come in, do come in. You must be Sarla – did you see your mum on Sky last night? I hope you didn't: it was so scary, all those guns going off. She looked so thin! Can't wait to see her when she comes to collect you. Haven't talked to her in years. How're you getting on in Daroga? Isn't it lucky you and Bina have each other. Don't look at this tip. I never do any housework. Let me turn down that music ... hurt your ears,

Sarla? It's called Carnatic, i.e. South Indian. Don't imagine Rita has brought you up on it. But world music's all the rage in Britain, isn't it?"

She spoke with a very posh, clipped accent, but her house was a bit like our flat. If the garden was a jungle, the inside matched it, and her, perfectly. Avalanches of cushions, nesting cats, abandoned slippers, tottering piles of books and magazines and a year's back issues of newspapers; cheeping birds hopping in cages and dead flowers sulking in vases. A peculiar smell, probably old vase water, hung about and dust, thick layers of the stuff, showed up in the bright mountain light that streamed through the windows.

I fished Socks out of my shoulder bag, in which it was peacefully curled up.

"What's that, dear?" Antonia asked maternally. "Oh, Dora, your kitten's come back to you! We thought the mountain monsters had got it." She put the kitten under the nose of a fat grey cat that was snoozing on a bolster. "Dora is named after my aunt, who looks just like her. Such a sweet face!" She tipped up the cat's chin for us to see.

I liked Antonia. She reminded me of Rita's eccentric friends: the painter, the novelist, the one who was a mistress of a famous politician; she darted from one topic to another so that it took a few seconds to catch up. All of a sudden she switched her focus on Bina and started to sing her praises. Such an amazing dancer! What a unique talent!

"My star pupil," Antonia stroked Bina's arm. "We keep it very hush-hush because Hira would throw a fit if he knew she was going to perform in front of an audience next week. He thinks it's all right in the privacy of my house, but she's starring in her school show. You are coming to watch, aren't you?" She went on without drawing breath. "I have to give you a lesson today, Bina, because I've been called away to Chandigarh tomorrow. Will it be all right if Sarla and Sidhartha watch? A kind of dress rehearsal."

Bina made a face. I didn't blame her – having a dance lesson in front of the two of us wouldn't have been my idea of fun, and I'm a show-off, which Bina definitely was not. But she had been brought up to be good and obedient and mind her elders and betters, and I hadn't. She pressed her lips together, sort of gritting her lips, and sat on a stool to tie on her dancing bells, which were rows of little brass bells sewn on to a wide leather strap. She pushed up the cuffs of her salwar so they became like pedal pushers, tied her dupatta across her chest like a cross belt (to leave her arms free) and went chink-chink across the parquet floor and bowed with folded hands to the statue of a dancing Shiva.

Antonia seated herself on a low stool, a wooden baton in one hand and called out the opening beat: "Ta-thai-thai ta, ta thai-*tut*, tha."

I'd never seen proper Indian dancing before (only bits of Bollywood nonsense) so I didn't know what to expect.

Bina began slowly, marking each step to the definite beat set by Antonia. Then, in a little while, Bina's rhythm changed. Her feet hit the parquet firmly and went faster and faster. It was dizzying to watch how she whirled and twirled. Her arms wove patterns, her fingers made pictures. She danced with the most amazing concentration and focus. I didn't know what it was about, but she was good. Then I started to see *how* good she was: there was harmony in her movements and wonderful grace in her limbs. She was showing different emotions in her eyes and her facial expressions: fear, love, tenderness, anger, impatience. Such a lot of passion hidden underneath that quiet dignity and poise!

That must have been what finally did it, because Sidhartha was looking all dreamy and moony and goofy. There was no question that he had fallen for her.

"Bravo!" he said, clapping wildly as if he'd just watched a cricket match. "You are amazing!"

"Isn't she just? That, Sarla, was the story of Lord

Krishna hiding from his mother because he'd been a naughty little chap stealing the butter from her kitchen. You did the *abhinaya* very well, Bina. That's the facial expression, Sarla. Just a few things…" and Antonia demonstrated how she wanted Bina to improve certain details in her routine. "Arm straight, no a bit more like this. Point the third finger up like this … crisper footwork here. That's it. Now, a mischievous smile, sort of teasing, at this point…"

Antonia ended the lesson. "Did Bina tell you about our little trip to the mountains next month? After Piloo comes back from Bangalore we're planning to visit my artist friend. He is a painter of traditional miniatures and only paints scenes from Lord Krishna's life. If the monsoon hasn't washed away the roads we're going to walk part of the way. Do you want to come with us, Sarla? You're welcome, too, Sidhartha – apart from the mule man you'll be the only guy on an all-girl expedition!"

He beamed with pleasure. "I would like that. Where exactly is the painter's village?" Antonia explained how we would get there and Sidhartha suddenly looked serious.

"But won't it be risky, travelling in the area where the Lib Front are supposed to be so active?"

"They won't harm us. I'm very well known in those parts, and I have loads of friends among the villagers. But don't worry, of course we won't take any risks – I have the girls to think about. I'll check in advance if it's safe."

She waved us off from the top of the steps leading to the road. "Don't forget Saturday! You'll be our cheerleaders at the recital!" The dogs rushed around barking goodbye.

I wanted to talk to Bina and Sidhartha about Antonia and Piloo's expedition to meet the artist, the painter of miniature pictures, whose name was Master Nandkishore. Would Nana and Nani allow me to accompany the others? Would they think it safe enough to let me go walking in the mountains? It might be a lot of fun; also no one in my school would have done anything like that, and I'm definitely into one-upmanship. I wanted to see how the local villagers lived, and to travel on a country bus: we might even meet those Liberation Front people! That would look great on my school CV and much more impressive than a safari in Kenya, or mountain climbing in Austria.

But Bina and Sidhartha had overtaken me, completely absorbed in each other. I could sense the electricity crackling between them and wondered if teenagers ever kissed in front of other people in India. I know it can be a bit gross at home, but apparently in India things like that were censored, even in films. I'd once touched my lips to Sam's quickly, so I don't know if that counted as proper kissing.

Bina had told me that Bollywood stars danced round trees and made "suggestive movements" (she'd demonstrated gyrating hips accompanied with pelvic thrusts!) to show they were hot for one another. Sometimes on screen the director showed the sea moving in the sexy way it does (of course) and that was meant to symbolize they'd Done It! She'd promised to take me to a Bollywood block-buster after her exams.

After we got home and Sidhartha had left, Bina and I sat in my room and talked for ages. Predict-ably enough, she was all coy about Sid; it would take a little time for her to get used to the idea that he fancied her.

"The timing's brilliant" I enthused. "We're go-ing to talk to Sidhartha about how to deal with Jeevan. Now that he's fallen for you, I'm positive he'll help." But she went on worrying. "If Jeevan has got my dupatta then he's going to use it against me, I know he will."

That night I lay in bed wishing Rita was around. I felt a tug inside me. I'd been seeing her on Sky News looking panda-eyed and desperately tired. She spoke to the camera about the day's casualties and a military convoy that had been blown up by the rebels. I saw pictures of orphaned children and crazy-looking soldiers. She was surrounded by danger. I sent up an arrow prayer for her like Elizabeth had taught me.

Bina, too, was in danger of a different kind. I tossed and turned, unable to sleep with whatif-itis. What if Bina just brazened her way through the present threat: ignored Jeevan, stuck it out in school, dug in her heels and refused to give in to her grandparents. What if she didn't have the inner strength to overcome her fears. What if she didn't become a doctor? What if she and Sid got married? Now that really would be something! A girl from a poor family, a very dodgy background, marrying into aristocracy; I wondered if that had happened before, and then I remembered Sidhartha's grand-mother, the trapeze artiste from Romania, wife of Signor Paolo who'd been defeated in a duel for her hand. But of course scandals happened all the time and were soon forgotten and buried. It was *now* we had to deal with.

Fourteen

BINA

I was concentrating on my social studies homework when Koshy Aunty leant over my shoulder to whisper confidentially, "Bina, that nice boy has fallen for you. He has been here so often. Nothing to be ashamed of, *beti*, don't worry about it, he is a lovely chap, but the princess is getting a bit nervous." I was shocked that she had so quickly put two and two together. What about my grandparents – had they arrived at the same conclusion?

No one could overhear us, or see my face, but I went all hot. Like I had prickly heat. It was true that Sidhartha was always at our place recently. Once he'd even picked me up outside the school gates but, thank God, no one was with me and he'd parked his fancy car round the corner.

Even so, I felt weak. "What did she say?"

Koshy Aunty laughed softly. "Yesterday at our bridge session in the club I noticed she was sulking. When I asked, 'Vidya, are you coming down with something?' she said, 'Dinkoo isn't studying hard these days.' Then she looked at me – you know that piercing stare – 'I think he's spending too much time with your girls.' After that she shut up, because Mrs Mehta and Mrs Khan were all ears. Don't get too involved, *beti*. I don't want him to break your heart, however nice he is."

But later, how could I help it when Sidhartha phoned to say he wanted to take Sarla and me on a picnic. I felt I was going to burst! Could I have imagined in my wildest dreams that the boy I had a crush on – someone so special – would want to be friends with me?

"Our chowkidar told me about a waterfall called Sikra, about eight miles' drive from here. Heard about it?" He paused. "I'll take the small car because the road is so awful. Did you know there's a little temple in the caves dedicated to the Bandit Queen of the Hills? I thought Sarla would get a kick out of going there. Lalloo told me that the country people take their sick there to be healed. It's supposed to have magical properties, which will be fascinating from a medical point of view, don't you think? I'm very interested in the power of suggestion and traditional forms of healing. What do you say? Shall we go on Saturday after your school?"

When I told her about the plan, Sarla started jumping up and down like a small kid. "Perfect, perfect! Just the chance we were waiting for. I know he's going to want to help you with Jeevan. We'll have lots of time to tell him and get good ideas."

All at once that that sinking feeling came back, like before an exam. If I told Sidhartha about my mother would he want to know me? Or would he walk away? The old memories of being sentenced to a life of misery threatened to return. I'd always be judged by other people. Would I ever be allowed to be myself? Would I ever be separate from my family history?

I was so thrilled about going out with Sidhartha that I didn't mind Sarla was coming too. Actually, I don't think my grandparents would have let me go on my own. As it was, my grandmother asked Koshy Aunty, "Do you want me to chaperone the girls?" And Auntyji pretended to look puzzled as though she had no idea what Lila meant.

But I was also in a turmoil about seeing the shrine dedicated to my mother, since I had heard people talk about it and the stories about miracle cures. I would be careful, I thought, not to reveal anything to Sidhartha. It was too early in our friendship.

* * *

Sidhartha drove carefully along a bumpy road that hadn't been repaired for years. He parked near a culvert and we took the steep path leading to the river below. It was hard not to lose my balance; thank goodness Sarla and I had on our trainers. We were more or less sliding on pebbles, trying to hold on to each other, when I heard the singing. It was faint, but I knew the song that floated up the gorge.

Devi Shobharani rey
Paharon ki bhi Rani
Devi Shobharani rey
Paharon ki bhi Rani.

Kawwey terey bhai bhatijey
Cheel teri darrani
Devi Shobharani rey
Paharon ki bhi Rani

"Listen!" Sidhartha held up a hand. It was a group of people climbing up the *pakdandi*, having been to the shrine. He translated for Sarla: "Devi Shobharani *rey* you are the Queen of the Hills. Crows are your brothers and nephews, the kite is your sister-in-law, oh, Shobharani you are Queen of the Hills."

Then we squeezed ourselves against the mountainside as the group trudged up our way: father, mother, grandfather and three children; they were poor folk from a nearby village. One thin little boy was shouldered on a stretcher, his legs all twisted; his mouth was also twisted and one side was wet with dribble.

Sidhartha greeted the family. "Ram Ram. Coming from the shrine?"

"Yes, sahib. We washed the child with holy water. Look, you can see he is very sick. We pray the great Devi will look on him with favour."

The grandfather had glasses with thick, badly scratched lenses, like old bottles. He peered at us, nodding sagely. "Yes, and the great Devi will come on the wings of an eagle. Then everything will be all right again. In the past she protected us – the rains came in time, we had bumper crops, cattle were healthy and people were strong and without fear."

The mother folded her hands reverently, "*Jai, Shobharani ki Jai.*" Hail to the Devi.

They continued their climb and we kept going downhill.

My mother! They had been talking about my mother. How they adored her, like she was a goddess in heaven! Suddenly I was reminded of Mary

Lobo's Holy Virgin. To these people, my mother is holy like Our Lady! I was overwhelmed with pride. She couldn't have been completely bad. She must have done a lot for others. These poor villagers would have been so happy if they'd known I was her daughter. They wouldn't have turned up their noses at me!

I would never forget that day. I felt so alive. I wanted to hug everything and everybody: trees, rocks, Sarla. I hummed "My Favourite Things," and I wanted to touch Sidhartha, hold his hand and tell him how happy I was. Colours were brighter than they had ever been, and the wind was singing in my ears. I could taste my happiness!

In this dreamy state, I skidded on a stone, tripped, and found myself caught in Sidhartha's arms. He was just a few paces behind, and he steadied me as I fell. Did I imagine it, or did he hold on to my hand a little bit longer than necessary? Did he press it?

Down in the valley, smooth grey rocks covered the bed of the river. The water was only a trickle, but when the rains came it would be a gushing torrent. I washed my hands in the cold water and looked around for Sarla. My heart was still thumping after Sidhartha's eyes and mine had met, so I was a little distracted. First I couldn't see her, but there she was, sitting under a tree. She wouldn't look at me and I realized her eyes were shiny with tears.

She said roughly, clearing her throat, "That poor little boy. He's never going to be cured with holy water. He's going to die, isn't he?"

"I think it's cerebral palsy," Sidhartha said coming up. "He needs a hospital and expert treatment."

"Stupid fairy tales." Sarla looked away over to the other side of the river bed. I was very touched by her soft heart. I sat down close and put my arm round her.

I said quietly, "That's why I want to become a doctor. This is only one case. There are millions and millions of sick people in our country and I want to help them get better."

Sidhartha said, "And me too," and it was just like he and I were in partnership in a great cause – something noble and bigger than either of us. Hope seemed possible now; change even more so.

Sarla looked up. "It's easy to say all that, Dinkoo. You'll forget it when you start working. Why would you want to help poor people like that? There can't be any money in it." She must have been very upset to sound so cynical.

He pulled his right ear, a habit that was becoming familiar to me.

"You know, thousands of years ago, the Buddha,

before he became the Buddha, was a prince named Sidhartha. All his life, Sidhartha had been shielded from all the painful and ugly sights of the world, but one day he saw a body being carried to its funeral and that was the day he started to think for himself, and to question the meaning of life.

"Listen, Sarla, just because I come from a princely family and a so-called posh background doesn't mean I'm into wine, women and song! Let me tell you a bit about myself, it'll put things in perspective. You say, why should I do something with my life that doesn't earn a lot of money? Well, the most important thing I've learned is to try and understand who I am. And what makes me deeply uncomfortable is having advantages, when all around me people are starving."

Sidhartha looked into the distance, then continued. "I hate being reminded of this big divide between rich and poor. I haven't had a happy or secure childhood – my mum died when I was nine and my dad – you heard Aunty Vidya mention him the other evening – just took off! He left my sister and me with relatives. Luckily Meera was already engaged to be married, and she took charge of me when she had her own home."

Sarla looked just a little ashamed of herself. "What do you mean your dad took off? Where'd he go?"

"Oh, he joined a commune and became a sadhu – a holy man. He lives in the mountains in an ashram. I haven't seen him for the last two years. Once when I was younger I asked him, 'Daddy, don't you care about Meera and me? Don't you worry about us?' Do you know what he replied? 'Does a mountain trout swim back to the glacier?'"

Sarla frowned. "Hmm, he sounds like a case, but what's your sister like?"

"Oh, nice enough; Meera's into Delhi society in a big way. They have pots and pots of money. Three kids, four cars, ten servants... Her husband makes sports gear and they go to the Delhi Golf Club, attend bridge parties, drink champagne – all the usual things. I can't stand their way of life, so I rebelled and started travelling by public transport and helping the servants in the house. My sister thinks I'm a Communist!"

"That's your guilty conscience," Sarla said, being rude again. Where did she get it from? I marvelled at her self-confidence. She really didn't care what people thought of her.

"Well, my grandfather may have been a maharajah, but he was a selfish, mean person. He never did anything to help anyone. It runs in the family, so maybe I want to break the tradition. All those wonderful rulers with their jewels and wealth, what did they do for their subjects? They robbed them! OK, enough family history. Come on you two, let's find that cave."

We crossed the river on a bridge of flat, wet stones and saw the cave with the shrine in front of us. Old marigolds were trampled into the mud outside. We slipped off our shoes and went in.

Sidhartha shone his torch on a crude figure carved into the rock, painted yellow and red. The idol's huge eyes looked beyond us. In front of her were clay saucers of rock sugar that were crawling with black ants. Heaps of fading flowers were scattered around. She carried a spear in one hand, and the other was held up, palm outwards. I had expected a gentle version of Our Lady, but this effigy was angry and glaring. Was this really how people saw my mother?

The smell of bat droppings made me feel sick. When I couldn't stand it any longer, I went out into the fresh air and took deep breaths to steady myself.

Sarla came out as well and pressed my arm. "Are you OK?"

"I'll be fine," I said, and I blew my nose.

"Hope we get good rains this year." Sidhartha was leading the way back to the car. He turned round. "There's always been a water problem in these parts, though you wouldn't guess it from the monsoon. Now here's a story. Ages ago, in the 1860s, the villagers begged my great-great-grandfather for money to dig a well." He paused. "They had been suffering a drought, so he did give money for a well, not to his own people, *but to a village in England*. His own subjects could have died for all he cared!"

Sarla stopped. *"What…?"*

"That's right. He wanted to suck up to the British resident during the Raj. My noble ancestor wanted a bigger gun salute – I think he was entitled to twelve, but he wanted more, so he was given seventeen by Victoria herself! Typical toady shoe-licker who wanted his tiger shoots, to be a big man with the viceroy, a favourite of the imperial power. That's what the Brits did to India. They made *our* country their toy, their pet, and milked it for everything they could."

"We did the Raj for a school project," Sarla said.

"Did you learn about our independence movement? Ask your Nani how she marched against the British in the thirties. It's quite a story."

We dangled our feet over the culvert and ate our picnic. Sidhartha picked wild yellow raspberries for pudding. Sarla had become very quiet for a change. She was throwing stones down into the gully, and finally she spoke. "Why does the goddess look so angry? How can you worship her when she looks as though she might cut you up into little pieces?"

Sidhartha thought for a minute. "Anger can also represent strength. The people who pray to her call upon her strength. The Bandit Queen was very powerful in her time, so powerful that simple folk see her power as a supernatural thing. Powerful people are always worshipped in India. Look at our politicians!"

Sarla chewed this over. "What do you think of Krishna? He's such a sweetie, isn't he? I love his naughtiness – and he was such a flirt."

Calling Lord Krishna a sweetie!

She went on, "Who's your favourite god, Sidhartha?"

Honestly!

"Don't know if I'm even a Hindu ... but I think that all the gods are different aspects of some universal energy – or something like that. I'm not the person to ask. I really don't know."

"I thought you were wise like the Buddha. You just told me that Sidhartha was the prince who became the Buddha. Did he find his princess before he got all holy and wise?"

Sidhartha couldn't help smiling. He started to gather the picnic things. It was time to leave.

I felt that if I didn't speak I'd choke. I had to say it, to get it off my chest. A mountain kite soared in the sky above us. *The kite is your sister-in-law.* It took all my guts, but at last I came out with it.

"Sidhartha, I have to tell you something. Something about my mother."

Fifteen

&

SARLA

I was very impressed by my mum's old school. All polished wooden floors and potted plants in shiny brass pots. It was obviously exclusive and expensive, of course. My grandfather only had his pension, so it was especially generous that he was paying for Bina's education. She would have had another kind of life if they hadn't been around to help her. I'd seen a government school from the outside and it was very different from the orderly, cared for environment of the Convent of the Immaculate Conception.

Nani told me about the missionary orders during the British Raj; some of the best schools had been started by Catholic orders – nuns for the girls and priests for boys. She said it was the done thing for children from "good families" to learn English from native speakers. "There was a down side of course. They grew up knowing much less about Indian culture than about the West. Look how English all this is…"

It was true; it reminded me of my school. Plaques with gold-lettered names of sporting triumphs, old head girls and principals lined the walls, together with coloured prints of Constable and French Impressionists.

Nani, Sidhartha and I had gone to see Bina dance at the Founder's Day function, and I noticed that the audience was incredibly glamorous. The women were dressed in gorgeously coloured outfits and jewellery and the men looked very posh in blazers and ties.

The assembly hall was crowded with rows of girls and their relatives. One girl recited Shelley's "Ode to the West Wind" with lots of feeling: clasped hands, hips swaying and eyes rolling. I couldn't help giggling, and Sidhartha had to pinch me. Another girl played "The Entertainer" by Scott Joplin on the piano, which was quite good. There was a one-act play where we were allowed to laugh properly and then Antonia turned on the tape of that gargling singing for Bina's dance.

I couldn't believe how beautiful she looked on stage.

She was made up with foundation and rouge and lipstick and her eyes were outlined with kohl, so they looked even bigger. She wore an outfit of peacock-blue silk and had flowers in her hair. Wow! Sidhartha's mouth fell open at the sight!

She bowed to a flickering oil lamp, and then she bowed to us, the audience. It was like the rehearsal at Antonia's. She started quite slowly, with small deliberate movements. It was her introduction. Then she started to dance the story of Krishna stealing the butter from his mother's kitchen. How did she manage to co-ordinate her arms and legs? Not to mention her fingers, which seemed to weave magic in the air. Her hennaed feet flew and when she got to the bit where Krishna begs his mum not to be angry, I actually could feel her fear; when his mum forgives him I felt his joy. I'd never known that dance was all about emotion – I'd always thought it was to do with skill and gymnastics. It made me want to dance myself! And I knew Bina had been in those places, deep down inside herself. She knew about fear and joy and love and longing. What's more, she knew how to make us share in them.

Everyone was riveted – you could see how they froze into a kind of dumb incredulity. Those snobby girls Bina had told me about … well, this would show them and their precious parents! Her great friend Mary Lobo was next to me, and she was grinning with pride and delight. She kept digging me in the ribs, but I didn't mind. I liked her because she was Bina's friend. As for Sidhartha, I couldn't begin to imagine what he was thinking.

I glanced sideways at him. Earlier that day, at Sikra Falls, after she'd bravely told him her story, he'd hugged her and was very subdued as we drove home after our picnic; but I just *knew* he wouldn't back off. In fact I think that was the moment that ended any dithering and made him decide that she was The One.

After the show I had to meet the principal, Mother Imelda Rosario, a nun from Kerala. Nani introduced me to Mrs Bannerji, the biology teacher known as Bio Banner and to Miss Merriweather. "Her mother is one of your old girls," Nani explained. Miss Merriweather was Anglo-Indian, but she wore a sari like the rest of them. "We would love to hear all about your English school, Sarla. Do come and give a talk." Miss Merriweather said in a singsong voice, "We hear moral standards are very low in the UK."

Another teacher chipped in, "Lots of Indian parents living abroad are sending their girls to us for an old-fashioned education. We don't allow any boys, drugs or alcohol."

"I'm not giving any talks," I told to Nani later. "It's my holiday."

"Think what it'll do for Bina, darling: prestige by association. If the other girls link her to you, it will raise Bina's stock. After all, you go to an English school and that gives you a certain cachet. They'd all love to be close to London."

After Bina's stage triumph Sidhartha took us for a drink at the club. "Can't offer you champagne, but the salted cashews are good and the Fanta is vintage." He had a nice sense of humour.

The club was crowded with summer holiday-makers. The women were very fashionably dressed in stilettos and slinky outfits, and the air reeked of French perfume and cigarettes. Heads swivelled when we came in, because everyone knew Sidhar-tha. I could read their minds: what is he doing with those two awkward teenagers in not-very-smart clothes? What are they to princess Vidya's hand-some well-born nephew? Probably poor country cousins ... or something like that.

When Sidhartha dropped us home, I saw Jeevan hanging around the gate smoking. He shielded his eyes from the glare of the headlights as the car swung into the drive. "Weasel-face," I said angrily. I quickly decided this was the time to tell Sid. I leant forward and prodded him. "Listen, we need your help. Bina is in terrible danger."

"What on earth do you mean?" He thought I was pulling a fast one, but he sobered up when I started the story. And we were able, at last, to offload on to someone who wouldn't go blabbing to my grandparents or to Bina's.

Sid was appalled. "You should have told me before. This is very serious. Look, let me sleep on it and try not to worry: I won't let that fellow do anything to hurt you, Bina. You know that, don't you?"

He squeezed her hand, blew me a kiss, and we went inside. Nani had been brought home earlier from the convent by some friends, and she and Nana were watching the news. He had stayed behind so that Hira and Lila wouldn't guess that Bina was up to something scandalous like performing on stage.

"Pity you couldn't see Bina," I whispered in his ear. "She was absolutely brilliant."

Nana winked. "So I heard from your Nani. Good for Bina!"

Sixteen

SARLA

I loved the hour or two after lunch when Nana and Nani snoozed on the verandah being just, well, *old*. It felt timeless in the warm sunshine, with the light pattering of the lawn sprinkler and birds calling outside. They'd start off reading their books (Nana liked history and spy stories) or else Nani would work on her bowl-of-grapes-and-oranges tapestry cushion cover. Then slowly their book or needle-work would fall on their laps or, with a soft plop, on to the floor and they were in noddy-land with their mouths open, a faint, faraway smile on their faces.

Lila also liked sitting in the sun on her stool knit-ting away. After a little while, she'd be dozing so there were three dear oldies dreaming away, with me flipping through *Femina*, until Bina got back from school.

The week after Bina's triumph on stage, Lila was showing me how to do a nice even plain–purl–stitch. Nana had gone somewhere and Nani had nodded off. Lila peered at my efforts. "Pull it tighter over the needle, or there will be gaps. The rains will soon be here and you will be happy to have a warm muffler to wear."

I could tell she was very pleased to have me to herself. She was much more demonstrative with me than she was with Bina. "Grandmother has never hugged me like she hugs you," Bina told me. "Honestly, I don't mind; I'm so used to it. I get lots of hugs from Koshy Aunty."

I felt bad about that, and it didn't seem fair that I had a double ration of hugs. During my clumsy efforts with the knitting needles, I daydreamed about this and that – my friends at home, Rita and Bina's many problems. In the background was a steady hum of bumblebees as they buzzed in and out of the petunias and dahlias. We still hadn't come up with a satisfactory plan to get rid of Jeevan without arousing suspicion (that did seem like the only solution: *get rid of* – as in *get him out of Daroga, and far away from Bina*). My mind wandered to other things. Now what had Sidhartha said I should ask Nani? I thought hard. Oh yes, about the time when she'd marched in a demo against the British.

Nani had finished her forty winks and her manicured hands, with their beautiful nails, were busy with the tapestry, so this was a good time to ask her.

"Nani, what was Sidhartha telling me about the independence movement against the British? He said you'd done something very exciting. Did you take part?"

She chuckled softly. "Just a very tiny part, my dear. Go and fetch the blue leather photo album on the shelf by Nana's desk and I'll tell you what happened."

She opened each stiff page carefully, smoothing down the transparent paper that protected the photos.

"This is me with your great-grandparents. Your great-grandfather, my father, was the prime minister of the state ruled by Princess Vidya's father, the maharajah. Now in those days the old king was a pretty powerful man and everyone had to do what he wanted. You know what feudalism is? Well, that's how he ruled his kingdom, with absolute authority."

Nani's father was a slight figure wearing a kind of frock coat and a great big turban with a fantail. Her mother sat stiffly on a chair with her head covered by her sari *pallu*. Round her forehead she wore a headache band, like I'd seen in photos of twenties' flappers. A potted palm separated them, and their children – Nani, looking like a doll with her hair in ringlets and wearing an organdie frock – sat on the floor with her brother and sister.

She showed me some more old photos of Princess Vidya's father, who I thought looked like an overweight frog covered in jewels. There was even one of his Romanian wife, Vidya's mother, draped round him. Then I saw Nani as a student at Khempur College for Women (Khempur was the capital of the state, whereas Daroga was the mountain retreat for the summer months).

She began her story, "So this is what happened: In nineteen thirty-two, when I was a student of seventeen, Mahatma Gandhi asked all Indians to boycott everything imported from Britain."

"Why, Nani?"

"To show that we could manage without – that we didn't need to be dependent on foreign-made goods. Through their long presence in India, the British had given us an inferiority complex: that we weren't good enough; that we couldn't do anything without their help or approval. Gandhiji wanted the better-off, educated Indians to live simply and not try to copy the British way of life.

"We students asked all the shopkeepers in Khempur to burn their imported stuff. The only one who was with us was Duli Ram chemist. He brought out all his Elizabeth Arden creams, his Bronnley soaps, Kent hairbrushes. Then lots of families joined in and we made a huge bonfire in the market square. In went teddy bears, porcelain dolls, fur coats and handbags and shoes from Bond Street!"

I tried to imagine the scene – a roaring bonfire, Nani and her friends chucking their precious things in it, and everything melting and disappearing in the crackling flames.

I jumped at the sound of crunching gravel. It was Sidhartha's car turning into the drive. He bounded in and I gave him a high five and whispered, "You're too early, she's not here."

"Got a bit bored with anatomy, so I came to keep you company for a bit."

He didn't see Nani giving him an "arch look" and he picked up the photo album. "Look how obese he was! My grandfather ate and drank too much. Sarla, here, I brought you a video of Richard Attenborough's film *Gandhi*. Nice, painless potted history about the freedom movement."

"Just what we were talking about," said Nani.

"Go on, Nani. Then what happened? You got to the bonfire…"

"Some tattletale ran to complain to my father: 'Koshy has joined the Nationalists. Come quick before she brings disgrace on your family!' So poor Papaji came running from his office, because he knew he could lose his job. Sidhartha, your grandfather, the maharajah, was *such* a buddy of the British that any connection with Gandhiji would have put them on red alert, as far as he was concerned. Papaji arrived in the market square to see me carrying a banner, 'Down with the British. India belongs to us! *Hindustan Hamara Hai!*' and of course he begged me to stop and come away. But I wouldn't listen, I was so fired up, with all my friends singing patriotic songs. Of course something terrible happened."

We waited to hear.

"Papaji was wearing his beautiful black sherwani coat and white trousers. Every day Mama had it sponged and pressed, spick and span. On his head he always wore a pink muslin turban that took half an hour to tie every morning. He lifted his turban and placed it at my feet! He was begging me to come away. He laid his honour at my feet. The shame of it, in front of the whole world!"

Nani looked down, and I think she couldn't help crying at the memory. "I never listened. I shouted, 'Go and tell your traitor maharajah that we want the British out of our country!' So Papaji left the market square, having been insulted by his own daughter. It was unheard of, in those days, to defy our elders.

We never showed them any disrespect."

"And then?"

"The inevitable: Papaji was sacked from the job he'd held for twenty years, and his father before him. He and the maharajah never spoke to each other again."

Sidhartha covered his face with his hands. "Oh my God. I knew he was a tyrant, but no one told me he'd done that to your father."

"Well, I suppose he didn't have a choice. Things were very black and white in those days. We had to sell everything. Our carriage, our silver, our land, mother's jewellery; all went to the auction house. The least I could do was try and make up the damage I had caused."

"How was that, Nani?"

"I gave up my dreams to become a doctor and agreed to marry your nana. He was a young lieutenant in the army. Luckily we fell in love after we were married so all's well that ends well."

"And you stayed friends with the princess, the villain's daughter."

"Oh yes, especially as she had such a sad life. Bunty – her husband – was an alcoholic. He was unfaithful, did all the usual, awful things: mistress in the south of France, racehorses, yachts. It was almost a relief to everyone, including Vidya, when he was killed in the Second World War."

"Phew, what a story. Why on earth has my mother never told me anything?" I demanded.

Nani ignored my question. She looked at her wristwatch, and my impression was that she said the first thing that came into her head. "There's still a little time before Bina returns – she has a late tutorial this afternoon. Can you take something for Antonia? We have some leftover chicken that I think she'd enjoy. She doesn't eat properly."

We trudged up to the The Nook with a steel tiffin carrier of chicken and that lovely buttery spinach called *sarson ka saag*.

On the way back Sidhartha glanced sideways at me. He was trying not to look smug. "I've got a fantastic solution to the Jeevan problem."

"Go on then, spill the beans."

"I'd rather wait and tell you both together. Do you mind? Let's go and meet Bina on her way back home. We'll walk into town, so we don't embarrass her in the limo. But, wait a minute, there's something else in the car I forgot."

We stopped by the gate of Stoneleigh and he ducked into the drive, returning with a book in his hand. It was bound and looked like an antique. When I opened it the spine creaked and I saw that it was a diary written in faded copperplate on cream-coloured paper. The pages were powdery and when I put my nose in the pages I smelt a heavenly aromar of tinned custard.

I read: *"Norah Everton Eames. My Diary. Do Not Read Unless You Have My Permission."*

"You must promise to look after it. It was written by a young girl who lived in our state around the end of the nineteenth century. In fact I think she and her family lived in Stoneleigh. She talks about the water well in England that I told you about, so I thought you might find it interesting."

"Thanks, Sid." I felt quite honoured that he was prepared to lend me what, presumably, was a family heirloom. "Can you put it in your satchel until we get home?"

He slipped it in the cloth bag, his *jhola*, that he always carried over his shoulder. Nana had told me that it was standard gear for arty types and lefties.

"By the way, just one thing, Sarla: I'd hoped you'd notice that I hate being called Sid. Or even Dinkoo. It makes me sound like someone out of P.G. Wodehouse or an Ealing comedy."

"Really? I think it's sweet. My mother calls me Poochi, when no one's listening. And do you think Piloo minds being called by her silly name? You know her real name is Purnima."

He clicked his tongue impatiently.

I went on, unrepentant, "It's so … Indian. Just like my mum's convent-speak."

"And I suppose you think Bina talks in a funny way too."

"So Ind-glish."

"Hilarious. And you are now being very patronizing and colonial."

I shut up.

Where our lane met the road coming from town it made a T-junction. The cantonment was a very quiet part of Daroga, so we didn't see anyone around. About a hundred metres before the junction a narrow goat track branched away from the lane into the forest. Bina had taken me down it once to show me a clump of wild raspberry bushes. Something caught my eye. A small white hanky embroidered with a little red rose.

"Sid, look! Bina must have come this way already. We've missed her."

He examined the hanky. "Where's she got to then?"

There was a loud and terrified scream from the forest.

"What was that? Come on, Sarla, let's go!" And we turned into the goat path and started running.

Seventeen

BINA

There was only a week to my mocks, and Bio Bannerji wanted to go over my work. I think she was fond of me because she always tried to cut at least one joke when I was with her, even if it wasn't very funny. Anyway, I like anyone who pays me attention.

"That was a beautiful show, Bina. You must keep up your Bharata Natyam when you go to university."

"Oh, Miss, do you think I'll make it?"

I knew I was her special project – the girl who was going to be a success against all the odds.

"If you can achieve that level of art in your dancing, then why not aim for the top in everything? Of course you are going to succeed. Remember, though, you must get ninety per cent in the mocks."

We discussed my biology paper and I started home, quite overwhelmed at the work I had to cram in this week. Straight after the exams Antonia was taking us trekking to meet Master Nandkishore, the painter who lived in the hills. Piloo would be here soon and after the trek it would be time to say goodbye to Sarla.

I didn't want to think about her leaving. It was so nice to have someone near my age to talk to and confide in. I'd started to trust her and think of her as a friend. No, even more, I had become quite fond of her. Besides, with her around I was free to see Sidhartha. Once she was gone, my grandfather was sure to start making a fuss.

As I was walking, lost in my thoughts, a rickshawallah pedalled slowly behind me. "*Behanji*, save yourself the walk. I will give you a ride. I haven't earned anything today. Only five rupees to take you home."

I shook my head. I hated being pulled by a rickshaw man. I felt sorry for them because many of them had TB and they coughed and spat on the road.

Sidhartha was sure to be at Stoneleigh. He said he'd try and get enough anatomy revision finished and was going to bring his textbooks to show me. Showing his books to me was always a good cover for a visit.

I just wished I didn't have that worry about Jeevan hanging over me. Maybe Sidhartha would have thought of something since our last meeting. I turned into the lane that led from the road towards Stoneleigh. I'd hardly walked a few metres when – horror – I saw Jeevan blocking my way.

"Madamji, excuse me. Just one minute please," he said mockingly in English, aping some film hero or other.

I kept my eyes on the ground and refused to meet his. "What do you want?"

"Nothing, nothing." He bowed in a mocking way with folded hands.

What was this drama all about?

"I have something of yours. Does this belong to *Your Majesty*?" and he held up the very same blue dupatta that I'd lost a couple of weeks ago.

"Where did you find it? No, it's not mine," I lied.

"Aha! I think your grandparents would recognize it. Not so quick, madamji. You'll have to come and take it from me. I wonder what your grandfather will say when I show it to him?" He danced and stepped sideways into the little goat track where Sarla and I had picked raspberries.

He kept skipping backwards, facing me, a few steps in front, waving my scarf above his head, teasing and making fun of my attempts to snatch it from him. It was such an obvious trap, but I wasn't thinking, so I followed him deeper and deeper into the jungle. My arms were scratched from thorns and I started to feel panicky. What if someone saw us in this lonely place? What would they think?

When we arrived at a clearing in the bushes. Jeevan suddenly halted and thrust his face up close to mine. "What have you decided? Are you going to say yes to marrying me? Or has your head been turned by that snob, Sidhartha? I wonder what he will say if he's told about your mother?"

"Don't worry, he knows."

I shouldn't have said anything.

"Oho, so it's getting serious, is it? Very intimate! I'll give that puppy something to think about," and he grabbed the front of my kameez. He pulled off my dupatta and tried to bring me close to him. I smelt his disgusting smell: cheap alcohol and cigarettes and my mouth filled up with sour bile.

My heart was thumping like an engine. He may have been skinny, but he was stronger than me, and he was trying to twist my head round so he could kiss me. Somehow I managed to free my right arm and whack him with my schoolbag. The strap was too long and the bag was too heavy and clumsy. He grabbed it out of my hand and flung it down so all my books spilt out. I don't know why, but at that point, suddenly, my mother's image came before me. I saw her clearly as the Devi, the goddess in the shrine, waving a trident with eyes flaming like a tigress. I don't know how I filled my lungs with air and started screaming, "*Devi, Devi, Bachao!* Save me!"

My screaming didn't stop him. He struggled furiously to hold me so I wouldn't wriggle when, seconds later, I heard someone crashing through the bushes towards us. I heard two voices chorusing, "We're here! We're coming!" and suddenly, like a miracle, there was Sidhartha, and right behind him followed Sarla, her mouth open and face white with shock.

"Get off, get off, get off, you miserable little rat!" Sidhartha gripped Jeevan's arm and slapped his face hard. He threw Jeevan to the ground and gave his backside a kick and turned to me. The three of us hugged each other. I was sobbing wildly. Jeevan tried to slip away in all the confusion, but Sidhartha grabbed him by the collar and brought him back.

"Sarla, take Bina to Antonia's. You'll have to tell her what happened, but ask her not to say anything to anyone. Not yet. This little worm won't be here much longer. Go on, you two, don't wait for me; I've got to do a few things with this creature first."

From the corner of my eye I saw him twist Jeevan's ear and as we left Sidhartha was shouting, "You are the scum of the earth and you deserve to go to the police. Shall we go to the station?"

Oh God, I thought. Not to the police, there would be a scandal and that was the last thing I needed.

"Come on, Bina, let me take your bag. Just lean on me and you'll be all right."

Carefully, holding my hand, Sarla led the way and we left Sidhartha to sort it out.

I babbled, "Did you hear me calling to my mother, to the Devi, and she came! It was a miracle, Sarla, a miracle. My mother flew on the wings of a kite and she saved me!"

Eighteen

❧

SARLA

Only a few hours after the terrible incident we both got sick, as in sore throats, fever and tummy aches. Bina had to keep going to the loo. I was the only one who knew the strength of her willpower in not letting on to anyone how wobbly she was feeling.

It played itself over and over in my mind: the little white hanky in the bush, Sidhartha's shocked face, running down the path, the bushes snagging my clothes and scratching my arms – the screams! And then the sight of her twisting and struggling in Jeevan's grip! His face – so close to hers – with him panting like a thirsty dog; then his expression changing when he caught sight of us. Sidhartha taking over, pushing Jeevan to one side and slapping him, his open hand like a cracking whip. I'd caught Bina as she'd stumbled and nearly fell, and

I'd hugged her as tightly as I could, my T-shirt very quickly soaked with her tears.

Every time I saw these scenes, my heart started to race. Poor Bina; she'd done nothing to deserve this. I grew hot with anger at the unfairness of it, and I thought that if anyone dared to do that to me, I'd kill him, I really would. And then I remembered that's exactly what Bina's mother had done – nearly killed her husband because he'd treated her like a thing, an object for his convenience. In a flash I understood why her anger must have built up and up and up, until she couldn't help herself.

I didn't know what had happened to Jeevan after that.

Antonia had comforted Bina and taken us back to Stoneleigh, after giving her a dose of Rescue Remedy and a cup of tea. "You must calm down, Bina. Hush, hush, remember your mocks are round the corner, and you need your wits about you. We're here to stand by you and make sure no one will harm you again."

But as soon as Nani saw the two of us, she said we looked feverish. She took our temperatures and tucked Bina up in the second spare room, next to mine, and we both slept through the night and nearly the whole of the next day.

I felt better the second day, but Nani wouldn't

let me get up. She propped me up on pillows and spoiled me. Lila brought me bowls of hot *kichdi*, and ginger tea in a mug.

Nani came and perched on the end of my bed. "This is the best nourishment for invalids: dal and rice boiled up together and mixed with a little ghee – very easy to digest. Look here's the latest *Eve's Weekly* and *Femina*. You can catch up with all the fashion news. I know how interested you are in those things!"

That afternoon Antonia brought news of Piloo. She was on her way to Daroga. She also had a message from Sidhartha. "He's got a brilliant plan to deal with Jeevan – in fact it's already in operation. He's had to go away to put him on a train … but I won't spoil it for Sidhartha. He'll tell you himself when he's back."

No amount of nagging would persuade her to go into details. "You must learn the art of patience, my dear!"

There was a short crackly call from Tajikistan. Mum could have been on the moon, she sounded so distant. All she managed was, "Are you all right? Having fun? It's awful out here…" and then the line went dead.

I flipped through the mags. They were very dull: all about recipes, cucumber slices for reducing dark circles and tips for keeping cool in summer. Only the agony aunt was funny. Her advice was always to be sensible and keep everyone happy. One woman had fallen for another man, even though she was engaged. Another had hair on her face and a third one had crazy parents. They worried she'd never find a husband because she was so short and made her hang with her arms from a jungle gym every day!

Dear Sonu
Your arms will grow longer, that's for sure! Why not try a simpler solution: wearing high heels? Do remember, India is full of short men. In any case men love petite women, as it makes them feel strong and superior. Good luck with husband-hunting!
   Sheela

Giggling, I went into Bina's room to read a selection of letters out to her.

"Shall I send Sonu my platforms?"

Bina just wasn't being silly. She couldn't understand why I found the letters so amusing.

"Go away, Sarla; don't bother me right now. I've got a headache, and I'm not in the mood."

I tried to get her to lighten up, with the good news about Jeevan chugging away from Daroga on a train. "Dinkoo's coming tomorrow to give us the details."

"Sarla, *please*. You know he hates that stupid name."

I looked at her bruises. She was keeping her arms under the covers so no one would notice. I went back into bed and started reading the creaky diary that Sid had lent me. I read right until dinner-time. When I finished the last page, it was like climbing out of a time capsule. For the last two hours I had been lost in another world and another century.

Norah Everton Eames.
My Diary
Do Not Read Unless You Have My Permission
No. 3 Barracks Road, Khempore, U.P. India, Asia, The World.

5 November 1860
A Guy Fawkes bonfire would be very unsuitable, because we are in mourning for dearest, most darling Mama and poor little baby Richard. The younger ones are very disappointed because Ayah's son brought us some sparklers from the bazaar. Papa goes about with a sad face. He took the maharajah on a shoot last week so we were alone with Ayah and our governess, Miss Symonds. I cried every night. Miss Symonds says I should be sent to school back home, otherwise I will

*become a junglee girl. She is going to speak to Papa about it.
I won't go! I won't leave the babies and dear Father all by
themselves with Her. I think she has a Dastardly Plan.*

10 November 1860
*Went to tea with the Rajkumaris, who are such spoiled little
princesses. The older one is almost eleven, but she has terrible
tantrums and hits her maids if they do not immediately do as
she bids them. I try hard to be friendly, but get on better with
the younger Princess Dharmendralakshmi Victoria, named
after queen Victoria. The maharajah, her father, must be in
love with the queen, because he has pictures of her all over the
palace. We ate Dundee cake and were taken for rides in the
palanquin. They have an English governess who is teaching
them to play tennis. Miss Symonds does not approve of their
governess. She says that she is a pushy little thing who came
out on the fishing fleet to catch a husband in the civil service.
Miss Symonds is much too old to go fishing (I think she is
35!) but she has her sights set on Other Things.*

15 December 1860
*Very cold. It snowed on the hills. I wore my fur tippet. Little
Blanche has a streaming cold and the doctor says she is deli-
cate. I fed her broth.*
    *Papa ordered the headstone for Mother's grave. It will be
a weeping angel in white marble and will be placed on her
grave in St John's churchyard in Daroga on the occasion of*

her birthday, on Midsummer's Day.

26 December 1860, Boxing Day.
Papa was pleased with his present: a felt bookmark. I made
Miss Symonds a picture from pressed flowers. Blanche got a
ribbon for her hair and Andrew had colouring pencils from
me. I knitted a pair of mittens for Christopher. We all gave
Ayah a new shawl and the other servants had money from
Papa. I had a book of stories, a new book of Songs Without Words *(piano pieces by Felix Mendelssohn) and a clip*
for my hair. Cook burnt the Christmas pudding. Still very sad
about Mama – I cry most nights.

I couldn't imagine my life without my mum. There
would be a hole that nothing and no one could ever
fill. Again, I thought of Bina's loneliness and her
feelings of being deserted. Then there was Princess
Vidya whose mum had died so young, and Sid's
mother too. And here was Norah, a child of the
Raj, motherless like them.

I read about Norah's uncertainty about Miss Symonds; her refusal to go to school in England and
her longing for May to arrive when they would
spend the summer in Daroga, in the mountains.
The Everton Eameses had actually lived in our
house, in Stoneleigh!

Norah wrote about the commemoration service

for her mother in St John's Church and the fixing of the weeping angel in the graveyard. Of course! It was the same tomb on which I'd surprised the old Tibetan woman! Then Blanche fell ill and had to be removed to the army hospital; Andrew broke his arm and Christopher was very slow at his books and reading.

3 May 1861
Christopher climbed into the lychee tree and gorged himself on fruit. He stuck a slippery white lychee into his socket, like a glass eye, and scared the babies and poor Ayah nearly to death. He was running around the garden saying, "Where's my eye gone? Oh, I have lost my eye." He was quite ill afterwards with stomach cramps, otherwise he would have been punished.

13 June 1861
Papa fears Christopher will never make the army. Miss Symonds said that maybe he should train for a respectable trade when he is older.
Papa is very very very busy with the maharajah most evenings. After his office work, he goes up to The Retreat and they spend hours poring over maps and plans. Apparently the maharajah wants to get a well dug as a present for the people of a village in the Chilterns, in Berkshire. They have no water in summer when the stream runs dry. Then the ladies of the

village have to walk two miles carrying buckets home for their washing and cooking.

Miss Symonds was sniffy about it. She is advanced in her thinking and Papa told me her brother was a Darwinian in England. Miss S. thinks if the maharajah wants to spend his fortune, he should look to his own people. When she goes trekking in the hills she comes back with stories of terrible poverty and disease.

"Mr Everton Eames, sir, as Political Advisor to His Highness you can surely influence him! His villagers are starving and full of consumption. They live in appalling conditions, even worse than their animals!"

I thought Papa would be annoyed that she was interfering in his affairs, but he only smiled and said he would try to do his best, but the old boy had a bee in his bonnet about this well in Stokely. He wanted to build a kind of oriental canopy over the well and plant a great orchard of cherry trees for the villagers' benefit.

"Of course, His Highness has his eye on a KCMG and a role in the next Durbar," Papa commented.

30 July 1861
We came back to Khempore on Sunday because the rains had started. The roads always get treacherous with mud and landslides. As a treat Miss Symonds allowed the monkey man to give a performance with his darling little monkeys on the verandah. Ayah said they were full of fleas, but Miss S. told

her that we were all descended from Hanuman. Ayah was
pleased to hear that she was descended from the monkey god!
The girl monkey was the bride and the boy monkey was the
groom. They made such a sweet pair.

22 December 1861
Papa called me to his study to inform me that Prince Albert
had died on December 14. "I am afraid She will never get
over it. The maharajah is devastated because he wanted to
show off the engineering involved in the digging of the Stokely
well. The prince was so interested in technical matters. His
Highness has declared a period of four weeks' mourning in the
state so we have go around with black crape bands."

10 February 1862
Miss Symonds and Papa are to be married. I am very happy
for them, but I should like to go away to England and con-
tinue my studies there.

Here the diary ended. I had read through three
years of entries and come to know Norah and Sid's
great-great-grandfather and the famous well. And
Norah and her family had actually lived in the same
house where I was reading her private diaries.

Families were so complicated! Always some worm-
holes, some little twists and turns and hidden secrets!
How naïve I'd been to think that I was missing out

on this idealized situation. I didn't really know what went on in Grania's family – or Elizabeth's for that matter. Maybe Grania's mum was an alcoholic, or her dad was having an affair. Maybe Elizabeth's father resented his mother because she made them all go to mass. Maybe her brother wanted to run away from them all. Maybe things weren't so green on the other side of the fence. So much for happy families!

Nineteen

BINA

What a bad week it had been! Keeping control of myself, and feeling so ill and feeble. When I got out of bed my legs were wobbly and my head swam. And all in the run-up to my exams.

I tried hard not to dwell on my experience. I had been molested. No, I had to face up to the fact that I had nearly been raped. Once I had said the word, once I faced what it meant, my fear vanished. I think if I had shut it out, trembled under the bedclothes, gone on crying, it would always have haunted me. But I made myself be very still and calm and I didn't talk much to anyone. I thought: this is what has happened, but I'm not seriously hurt and I've come out the other side. No one, but *no one*, is ever going to lay a finger on me in that way again. Never will I be afraid of anyone.

What helped me was knowing that Jeevan had been sent somewhere far away. I couldn't have managed without Sarla's support. She was the steady ground under my feet.

Uncleji said, "Useless fellow. We'll have to look for another driver. The bloody scoundrel has just disappeared without any notice. Hira thinks he's found a job in Bombay. Well, good riddance. I never liked him." If only he'd known how much of a scoundrel Jeevan was!

My exams began on Thursday. On Wednesday night, who should arrive together in a taxi from the train station but Piloo and Sidhartha! They had travelled on the same train. Piloo had flown to Delhi by Indian Airlines from Bangalore, caught the Shatabdi Express and found she was travelling in the same compartment as Sidhartha who, of course, had been away dealing with Jeevan in Delhi.

As soon as we had Sidhartha to ourselves, Sarla said in her direct way, "You look like the cat that ate the canary, the cream and everything else. Hurry up and tell us happened with Jeevan – we're dying to hear."

It was true, he did look very pleased with himself.

"Even before you went through that horrible experience, Bina," his eyes were so kind, "I had a master plan to deal with Jeevan. I was going to tell both

Sarla and you when you got back from school that day. Just the night before, my sister, Meera, had phoned to say that Deepak (her husband) was in the middle of a big staff crisis. She asked me to enquire at the club and see if I could find any waiters, or any of the staff, who might like to go to Dubai and work in Deepak's sports factory. They would have to sign on for four years, but they'd be well paid with long leave after two years. It came to me in a flash: that's what I'd do with Jeevan!"

"Brilliant!" Sarla and I said together.

"After I sent you to Antonia's, I made it clear to Jeevan that he had no choice. If he didn't take up my offer he was in serious trouble with the police for attempted rape. There had been two witnesses so he didn't have a hope in hell." He slapped his hand on one knee. "Do you know his only interest was how much money he would earn! I suppose like everyone else he'd pictured the gold-paved streets of Dubai. I took him to Delhi by train and stuck to him like a leech. Next day Deepak interviewed him, signed him up – with a little pressure from me – and put him on the first plane to Dubai. It took a little time to arrange the passport and visa, and I didn't let him out of my sight. And that's it, he's gone!" Sidhartha struck his hands together, dusting off Jeevan for good.

I stared at him in a daze, hardly daring to believe my luck. I knew for certain Jeevan wouldn't bother me again. I knew his kind. He'd soon become immersed in his new life and his new toys. He would buy gold for his mother and a TV for his father. He would be saving more money than he dreamed of earning as a driver in India.

"What sort of work has Jeevan got?"

Sidhartha gave a wicked grin, looking even more pleased with himself. "Cleaning toilets in the factory! Deepak called it service facilitator."

We all laughed. Then, I couldn't help myself. I grabbed Sidhartha's hands and squeezed hard, thanking him but not being able to say a word. The next thing he had his arms round me!

Sarla pretended to scold us. "Stop it, you two, where's your common sense? Oh gosh, I think Hira's at the door! You're in BIG trouble..."

But I felt completely safe, and so happy. "What are we going to do now?" I asked, my head on his chest.

"Nothing. You are going to get top marks and then we're off for three days, trekking in the hills. We are going to celebrate!"

Antonia was the leader of the expedition, which consisted of Piloo, Sarla, Sidhartha and me.

It was good to see Piloo again. She had seen her guru perform some more miracles. "Oh, Sarla," she'd cried, "there's a wonderful blue aura round you. You look so well and so grown-up." Sarla winked at me.

Each of us carried a rucksack with two changes of clothes, a pullover and lightweight raincoats. Piloo took her father's big black umbrella. Her pigtail was very straight, her mouth very serious and her face very pale and still.

"I hope you don't mind my saying so, but I think we're taking a big risk. The rains have already started and just because this week is forecast dryish, it doesn't mean much."

Sarla rolled her eyes. She said what sounded like "Eeyore", but I didn't know what it meant. Sarla explained, "He's a donkey in a children's book who's always down in the dumps." It still didn't make sense.

Though Piloo is her best friend, Antonia got impatient. "Oh, *Piloo*, you're such a pessimist. We are not going to the high Himalaya, you know. We're in the foothills and there are lots of places to shelter – there's a village or hamlet every few miles."

"I'm not worried about rain, Toni, it's landslides and rocks and…"

"If you look like Eeyore your parents will stop

us going. They've already discussed the safety issue with their friend the ex-police commissioner. The police and army have just brought in the leader of the guerrillas from the badlands. They've arrested the brains behind the operation, so there's nothing to worry about on that front!"

"Who's that? What do you mean?" Sarla asked.

"The Liberation Front. Oh pooh! So many villagers know me," Antonia went on. "I've been wandering around for years – ever since Ashok and I went trekking on our honeymoon."

"Ashok, who's Ashok?" demanded Sarla.

"My husband, who was in the army. He died in a jeep accident. And since you're bound to ferret it out, Sarla, your aunt Piloo and I both went out with him. He couldn't chase Piloo to London, so he settled for me. It's rather nice that we both have his memory in common, isn't it, Piloo?"

We caught a country bus from the bus station in town. It was being loaded with bulging sacks and tightly corded parcels. A man standing on the roof stacked our rucksacks securely in the luggage carrier and ran a tarpaulin and rope over the lot. I had a window seat with Sarla next to me and Sidhartha put himself right behind us. The bus quickly filled up with people, carrying chickens and ducks in covered baskets, or babies tightly wrapped and wearing woolly hats. It was very noisy and everyone was excited to be going home to their village.

At last the driver revved up the engine and we were on our way.

Sidhartha leaned his forearms on the back of seat to talk. He pointed out interesting things in the landscape, and after a little while the old lady next to him couldn't hold in her curiosity. She nudged him with her elbow and showed two fingers joined together to express a pair. "You and she are married?" She jerked her head at me and the gold hoop in her nose went swinging sideways. I was so embarrassed.

"No, Maji, not yet" Sidhartha said laughing.

I could understand the old lady's confusion. Who had given permission to a young girl to openly laugh and joke with a young man? What were her mother and father thinking of? "You should get married soon," she advised him. "May the Devi bless you with lots of children."

Oh God, where was I going to hide my head? Sarla started to giggle.

Sidhartha cleverly turned the talk in another direction. "Which Devi do you worship?"

"Oh, we have many," and she named some of the local goddesses and then to my shock I heard my mother's name, Shobharani. "Yes, yes, the Queen of the Hills, *Paharon ki Rani*. She will help you. Where are you children going? Why are you travelling so far?"

"*Maji*, we are to going to see a friend who lives in a village called Rewari. We are going with our aunties."

"But it is many miles from Khera. The bus stops at Khera. How will you walk so far? You are city children."

"We have a couple of mules waiting for us in Khera. You know Kishenchand the mule man? His mules will carry our baggage."

"Kishenchand? Of course I know him. He is my husband's cousin's nephew. Where are you meeting him?"

"At the tea shop."

"Good, well it's right behind my house. First of all you and the *behanjis*," she nodded towards Antonia and Piloo, "must stop at our place and have something to eat."

Suddenly the bus pulled up sharply, and nearly everyone trooped out to do their business by the roadside. The men stood with their backs to us and the women just squatted by the ditch and covered their faces.

Sarla found it very funny. "Look, they're just

peeing away and they think it's fine because their faces are hidden under their dupattas!"

"You could copy them; here's my scarf," Sidhartha started to unwind his muffler.

"No way. I'd rather die."

I wasn't sure about stopping at a stranger's house, but the others were in a carefree and adventurous mood. I could imagine what this old woman's place would be like, dirty and full of flies, but I kept my mouth shut. Sidhartha kept on asking questions; he was like Sarla in this manner. I was brought up to be quiet and not be noticed, but I was learning that the more questions one asked the more people talked, and the more information one got. It was more interesting than keeping one's thoughts to oneself – like when two stones are rubbed together they make sparks.

"What is your biggest problem?" Sidhartha wanted to know.

"Water. Look, you can see around you. Look at the hills – they are dry like a desert and the only trees that flourish are wild apricots."

We peered out of the filthy windows that were streaked with vomit. (I noticed that country people don't travel well.) What she said was true – the hillsides were bare. Our geography teacher, Miss Merriweather, had explained the effects of soil erosion:

the more you cut trees for fuel, the more rainwater washed away the good things in the soil.

"We can scarcely grow two crops a year. Unless the Devi blesses us with rain, and that doesn't happen every year."

"Which Devi is that now?"

"*Paharon ki Rani*: the Queen of the Hills, of course."

Oh my God. They actually believed my mother sent them rain from heaven!

Sidhartha leant forward. "Sarla, you've heard about tree cover and how tree roots prevent rain from denuding hillsides. Do you know the legend of the god Shiva's Rasta hairstyle? In any poster or picture there's a fountain of water shooting from Shiva's head, which is the River Ganges. His matted hair is like the roots of trees holding the waters of the sacred river as it trickles down. So even the ancients knew the importance of tree roots for water."

After the three-hour journey, the rusty old bus pulled up in Khera village. Antonia's sharp eyes soon spied Kishenchand the mule man. He was sitting in the dark tea shop slurping up tea from a saucer. He pulled his tweed jerkin closer over his chest and hurried over on bendy bow legs. In both ears he wore gold hoops and he had a toothless but friendly smile. He offered us tea, but the old lady from the bus elbowed her way forward.

"Tcch! Not this filthy place! They are coming to my house to eat something." She picked up Piloo's rucksack and beckoned us to follow her. Kishenchand took his mules, Balu and Bhanu, by their bridles and obeyed his aunty-many-times-removed.

By now everyone was dying to go to the toilet. It was sure to be a hole in the ground, but even that was better than looking for cover in the village.

We found the old lady's husband lazing on a bed in the sun smoking his hookah. She shooed him up and got him cutting onions and garlic while she prepared vegetables and rice, and in no time everything was ready for us to eat.

The bathroom wasn't too bad – just a bit smelly. Like most village houses this was made of wood and mud. The husband and wife lived upstairs while the goats and chickens were downstairs. In the corner of one of the upstairs rooms was a small shrine with flowers and incense and a clay goddess who might have been Lakshmi. Near her, stuck to the wall, was a large coloured poster of my mother on horseback, a bit like Rani of Jhansi. I smiled to myself and stood for a few minutes saying a prayer. I didn't want to draw attention to the poster, so I didn't mention it to Sarla or the others.

My mother had become more real to me than she had ever been before. I felt her power and protection and I could see what an important figure she was to many simple people. Since the day she saved me from Jeevan, my anger against her had weakened and I was more at peace. I was full of pride and a feeling of possibility for the future. If she had built a name for herself from nothing, then so would I – my own destiny, my future, my life. The familiar tightness in my throat had dissolved, as though a demon was gone, leaving my body light and free. I was happy for the first time in my life – and I knew Sidhartha was partly responsible for this.

Antonia pressed some money into the old lady's hands. "For the Devi," she told her.

The old lady cackled. "She will come again. The prophecy says she will burst through the walls of the prison and come on the wings of the kite and her brother the crow. She will save us and make our crops grow tall and strong. She will heal our people. Hail to the Devi!"

"*Jai!*" we chorused back.

Sidhartha helped Kishenchand load up the mules and we set off for Rewari.

Twenty

His father would often creep into his thoughts.

The watchman, Sadhuram, rolled his memories around his mind, savouring them like delicious morsels. How useful he had felt when he was a boy; the vital link for the gang between the village and the fort. The gang had numerous hideouts, but in the end they always came back to Ghata, and it was within its ramparts that they finally perished. He knew that his father, Beharilal, loved him. He couldn't stay away from the boy for too long a time. And how well the son repaid the father's love: with pride and duty, running errands and carrying messages. His mother knew that her husband loved Shobharani, but she had accepted her role as the forgotten wife with dignity and never spoke against the chosen one to her son.

His family had suffered after Beharilal was shot dead. He had given his wife sufficient money for the boy's education and Sadhuram finished his schooling before going to college in

Ambala for a year. There he met his next hero and mentor, the prof. In fact, Prof was not a teacher but a post office clerk who had lapped up his Marx and Lenin. When he joined the Liberation Front at its inception, he took on the task of recruiting youngsters eager to be part of the new movement.

Sadhuram would have leapt from a mountain-top if the prof had asked him to, but since his arrest, his leader's wings had been clipped. There was no father figure to guide him, to plan strategy or lead the boys to battle.

The hills had never seemed so lonely and so silent. Sadhuram looked across them at the distant view from another safe house near Rewari. He tried his utmost to see into the future. He was empty of ideas, empty of feeling and empty of hope. He sucked a pebble and tried to think.

Purulia had been a major disaster and now prof, their C-in-C, had been ambushed by Special Branch. Two lads had also been taken. Prof had gone down to Daroga to meet a contact and been recognized, in spite of his disguise.

Sadhuram pondered his options. Should he hang on with the others until Prof escaped from custody? (Among his many talents the prof boasted a fantastic skill in hypnosis.) Or should he lay plans of his own and try and raise funds by one of the emergency schemes on file?

Manoj had good connections in Khera village; Tiny could be relied on for procuring food supplies; Dhiraj could go to Ambala and see if the Eastern Unit would allow them temporary shelter and direction. Or should they wait in their present hideout until Prof got word to them? Sadhuram shuffled his options like a pack of cards, but couldn't see an obvious solution.

Morale had never been so low among the young men. So many in their unit had been captured in the last month. They were on to their last sack of rice. Sadhuram hardly remembered the taste of meat or eggs. Three of the boys were sick with dysentery and all of them felt lost without direction and leadership.

The Liberation Front was spread out all over the state. Their dream was to bring justice for the poor farmers who watched the rest of the world get richer while they starved. The suicide rate among the debt-ridden villagers was a scandal. They had not enough money for seeds, for manure, for implements and they received rock-bottom prices for their produce. Eventually they hoped to bring about a revolution in the hill villages so that people would be given their own state, separate from the existing one. It would be known as Pahariana – the Land of Mountains. Their goal was to highlight their own regional identity and institute a level of fairness for everyone.

Force was the only way forward. The Naxalites, who had similar aims, were creating havoc in the east of India and Nepal. The central government was genuinely nervous about that movement. One day they would sit up and recognize the Liberation Front as well.

By the end of the afternoon Sadhuram had decided to stop dithering and take matters into his own hands. He called an emergency forward planning meeting.

Twenty-one

&

SARLA

Cautiously I waggled arms and legs to see if my bones were rattling after the bus journey. That rust bucket would have failed its MOT without any problem. Bits hanging off the bodywork, obscenely gaping innards, huge clouds of black diesel belching like an old factory stack. The driver kept a cigarette permanently clamped in his mouth and turned round in a friendly way to chat to anyone who came up to the front. When he braked we nearly fell off our hard seats. When he went round hairpin bends I closed my eyes and gripped Bina's arm. Once he nearly ran over a woman carrying a load on her head. She clutched it with one hand and grabbed a child with the other. She looked as if she'd been plugged into an electrical socket.

Rewari was just ten kilometres from Khera, which

was far enough for me. I'm not keen about exerting myself (the time I went on a walking holiday with Elizabeth I thought I would *die*). After that journey I would have walked to the ends of the earth rather than get on another deathtrap bus.

Khera, where the bus had dropped us, was in the middle of a valley covered with fruit trees and rice fields, and now we were going to climb higher. The sun was bright after a rain shower and the terraced fields sparkled fresh and green. We started by walking alongside a wide river bed covered with grey boulders until suddenly a flock of goats materialized on the path. Sidhartha and Bina were walking hand in hand in front – no worries now about showing their feelings – while Antonia and Piloo chatted earnestly about gurus, meditations, mantras and other fascinating topics. Since I was last in the procession, I didn't have to keep up with the others and I dawdled a little, enjoying the vast sky and the sound of the water.

The goats crowded us and a goatherd tried to keep them in order with a switch. When he came up to us he chanted, "One-two-three-four-*five!*" I replied, "Testing, testing!" and we grinned at each other. His little sister followed him with a huge bundle of brushwood on her head. She couldn't have been more than six, but was already working for her family.

We turned a bend when Sidhartha shouted back to me. "Hey, Sarla, SOS – on your guard! Hide your eyes! Naked man on the rocks!" He pointed out a man cross-legged on a rock next to the water dressed in his birthday suit, which was blue-grey in colour. Apparently he'd rubbed wood ash all over himself. He sat still as a statue, but opened his eyes as we passed and they were red.

"Hash," Sidhartha explained. "Sadhu, holy man. They hang around these parts: lots of ashrams, free food, drugs, Westerners coming for enlightenment, so these guys cash in on their exotic expectations. My dad's holed up in an ashram looking for Nirvana. He hasn't made it easy for himself, or for Meera and me. I've met his guru. He's a fat little guy with bad teeth and a taste for pretty girls."

I sniggered. "Have you seen Piloo's guru? The one with eyes like fried eggs?"

Sidhartha made a gagging sound, but quietly, so he wouldn't be overheard by the aunties.

We started climbing until we were nearly 2,500 metres high. Kishenchand made a fire and brewed up tea in a kettle. We fell on a packet of Glaxo biscuits. I was starving and already missing Hira's sponge cake.

Soon after, the trees changed to evergreens and we smelled the wood smoke in our nostrils drifting down from the first houses of Rewari village. My legs were starting to buckle when we arrived at the Forest Rest House, which was to be our home for the next few days.

"Ashok and I came to this rest house on our honeymoon."

I was helping Antonia with the fire in the living room while Piloo and Bina made the beds. We were in three bedrooms, all very simple, which opened on to the front verandah. Each bedroom had its own bathroom, which was equally spartan, and Antonia told me that the water had to be heated in the kitchen in a galvanized metal container on a wood fire. Instead of proper toilets we had to use commodes because there was no sewage system, and the enamel toilet pans were cleaned by a sweeper every morning.

Antonia said airily, "It was just like this in Europe until a hundred years ago."

I wasn't looking forward to using one, but it was better than squatting in the garden.

The food was also cooked on top of clay ovens in which the chowkidar burned coal and wood. Antonia knew him well, and she discussed the menus for the next few days. "Yes, yes, memsahib. Plenty of fresh chickens."

Precisely. I'd heard them clucking in the back.

There was a scrabbling sound from the verandah and tapping on the windows. A crowd of happy faces were waving to us. Antonia knew the name of each child. She picked up the youngest and exclaimed how much she had grown since her last visit. "Aunty, Aunty," they chorused and she distributed the sweets she'd brought for them.

At last it was time to eat. We sat down at a table covered with a worn cloth and battered old cutlery. Dinner was a big bowl of steaming yellow dal and a platter of local rice. Piloo passed round a jar of mango chutney that she had brought in her luggage. For afters the chowkidar had put together powdered custard and tinned fruit, but everything tasted delicious. The chowkidar drew the faded chintz curtains in the bay windows with some ceremony, and with the botanical prints and sagging flowery armchairs we could have been in a shabby cottage in Somerset.

Antonia said, "I always feel a bit homesick for England when I stay here. The British set up a very good forestry department in India, and dozens of rest houses were built for their inspectors. It's funny how they're still going, fifty years later. You'll see the garden in the morning – full of English country flowers: hollyhocks, godetia, larkspur, dahlias."

"But they looked after the forests for their own

ends, didn't they?" Sidhartha put in. "They used the timber from India to lay railway sleepers in Britain, build ships and all sorts of other things … basically they just stole our resources."

"Not completely fair," Antonia interrupted. "British foresters also classified plants and conserved woodland in a scientific manner. It was never black and white. They took, but they also gave." She had adopted India, but hadn't given up her county accent or her loyalty to the country of her birth.

"Yes," sighed Piloo. "They gave us all the things that make up civilization – post and telegraph, convent schools, railways, tunnels, roads, bridges. What favours didn't you bestow on us natives, Antonia?"

Bina slept soundly, but I was too cold and had to cover my head with blankets. I'd always wondered why people wore those frilly caps at night and now I knew.

Breakfast was very "English" – porridge, toast, marmalade and tea – and afterwards, feeling very full, we strolled towards the village. The chowkidar's smallest children skipped along with us; the older ones had gone to school.

"Oh, the smell of the hills! It makes me so nostalgic…" Antonia sniffed the mossy green smoky air. "We're going to Master Nandkishore's after lunch so let me give you a guided tour of the village."

There wasn't a lot to see – a very poor collection of houses with very poor people living in them. They were two-storeyed, made of brick, mud and wood and many of them had blue painted beams and front doors. There were a couple of tea shops with huge blackened kettles and rough wooden benches on which men were idling, spending time smoking and gossiping.

"This so-called activity is called 'time-pass'. Women do most of the work in the fields, in addition to looking after the house and family. How old do you think she is?" Piloo pointed to a bent figure struggling up the lane with a pile of brushwood on her back.

"Fifty?"

"Wrong. No more than thirty. She's probably got four or five children and is coming back to cook the meal with the wood she's gathered."

"That pile won't last long," Sidhartha remarked.

"They have terrible problems finding fuel. Someone needs to invent a stove that'll last all day on four pieces of cow-dung. One of my friends in Tower Hamlets is working on the problem, and as you can see the villagers just go on living as though they're in the Middle Ages."

"Yes, they don't have great expectations, thanks to their local politicians," said Sidhartha.

Antonia, meanwhile, was hailing everyone with warm hellos and exchanging news with them. "That fat person there is the moneylender. I wouldn't give him the time of day, but I pretend to be friendly because if one of my friends is being pressed to pay up I can plead on their behalf."

"They need a simple banking system, don't they. Like that man has started in Bangladesh." Sidhartha was looking around, taking a keen interest in everything.

"And a village clinic," added Bina.

"And a village clinic, with a doctor and nurse," he echoed.

They weren't holding hands any more, because it would have looked very immodest and bizarre to the villagers. I noticed that the women walked a few paces behind the men, who were top dogs even when they lounged around more than their fair share.

Actually I was now finding it more difficult to think of Sidhartha as "Dinkoo". Maybe he deserved rather more dignity in his position as Bina's knight in shining armour. How odd that one could change attitudes so quickly, I thought. Not so long ago I was teasing him with his ridiculous nickname, and now it felt all wrong.

We stopped at one of the shops to buy matches

and candles. "Never know when the electricity will give up," said Antonia. "Sometimes for days. At least we'll be able to see in the dark."

I was astonished to see how simply the villagers lived. The shop only had basic things: rope, salt, lentils, rice, lumps of raw brown sugar, peanuts, lanterns, bars of red Lifebuoy soap, strips of chewing tobacco, biscuits in a glass jar, orange-coloured boiled sweets. The radio was playing those wailing film songs that you heard everywhere, a slimy drain ran outside and three little children played knuckles with pebbles in the dust.

After our chicken curry (tough as boots) and rice we flopped on the Forest Rest House verandah. At four o'clock it was time to set off once more for the village and our appointment with the artist.

"I won't tell you anything about Masterji. Let his pictures speak for themselves. It's such a special experience meeting him that each one of us will see something unique. It will be most interesting to compare notes afterwards."

Antonia stopped in front of a two-storey house, not far from the village shop where she'd bought matches and candles. She tested the first rough tread and started up a rickety open staircase that went straight from the lane to the first floor. A verandah ran all along the first floor with two doors leading to rooms; but a sudden explosion of angry shouting nearly caused us to tumble down the stairs. The door was open so we could hear everything, and though I couldn't understand a word it was obvious that a violent quarrel had erupted in Master Nandkishore's studio.

Antonia turned round, a finger to her mouth, and stopped us going up any further. Angry shouting and the noise of things being hurled around poured down the stairs.

Piloo whispered, "Should we see if Masterji is all right?"

There was another round of bitter-sounding words and someone flung himself out of the room. A young man of eighteen or twenty with a red bandana tied round his head and thunder written all over his face ran downstairs. He pushed past us and ran off down the lane.

Twenty-two

BINA

I hadn't been able to understand every word of the hill dialect, but before the strange man ran downstairs, I knew something was seriously wrong: one angry voice, the other murmuring softly. Sarla was watching my face, trying to interpret every wince and jerk that revealed my response to the harsh words. The dialect was too difficult for them.

"Uncle, you have gone senile – mad! Have you no sense of proportion? No care for money? Here I am, begging for scraps of food for the boys and you are merrily donating your valuable paintings to these foreigners! They will fetch thousands on the open market. I will sell them, no problem, in Delhi."

Then Masterji's voice seemed to be trying to calm his nephew, without success.

Masterji's voice had grown louder and agitated. He had told his nephew to leave since his guests were about to arrive.

"I don't want to stay! I don't want to be polluted by their presence. You can keep your wealth, your pictures, my inheritance…" That was the point at which he stamped out of the room and came running down the stairs, nearly colliding into us.

Masterji now came out. His looked very sad and bowed and when he saw us. He was embarrassed. He was tall and thin with shoulder-length white hair that curled at the end and wore a simple hand-spun brown *kurta* and white pyjamas. A muffler of local wool was knotted round his neck.

"What can I say, my friends?" He apologized in a low voice. "I am grieved by the young. They have their own ways and I cannot understand them. They have energy and fire – I would not like to change that – but wisdom and balance are so sadly lacking. Come, you are most welcome. Anjaliji, I have looked forward to your visit and this scene had to happen today! I wish you had not witnessed it."

Antonia was a little dazed by what had just happened, but she smiled warmly at him and introduced each of us. When she came to me she said, "My best pupil: an artist from the depths of her being. She is going to be a doctor. *Doctor banay gi*."

It was said with certainty, which pleased me.

Masterji looked at me with sharp-sharp eyes, almost as if he knew me. "You are an old soul. If you succeed in your ambition, you will be a healer of healers and twice blessed." I felt myself blushing. The compliment made me feel very honoured.

Then one by one he started to show his paintings. They were all about Lord Krishna and so beautiful that they went straight to my heart. The colours were the colours of a rainbow after a storm – pure and singing.

Antonia explained for Sarla's benefit, "When Lord Krishna was born, the evil king Kamsa dreamt that the god had come to destroy him, so he ordered the baby to be killed. Here, Vasudeva, the father of Krishna, is taking his newborn son to the house of Nanda and Yashoda who will bring him up. Doesn't it remind you of the story of Moses, or when baby Jesus was taken to Nazareth by Joseph and Mary to escape the wrath of Herod?

"This next picture shows Vasudeva returning home with Nanda and Yashoda's daughter, who will be brought up by him and his wife.

"Here we see Lord Krishna teasing his beloved Radha, the milkmaid. The maidens are bathing in the river and you can see the naughty god has hidden their clothes!

"Now here is one of Krishna being punished for stealing butter from his foster mother, Yashoda. Look, she's tied him to a tree, but he pulls it down and out fly these heavenly creatures from the branches! She is glancing out of her kitchen window to see what the noise is about."

Sidhartha touched my arm. "That was the story you danced, Bina. Look how Masterji has shown so much passion and movement in this scene. Krishnaji is dancing like you danced that night."

Once more I felt very honoured that I was being praised so much.

I looked around the studio, but there was nothing remarkable here except the pictures. Masterji painted on small pieces of old paper that he pasted on a wooden board. He explained his methods.

"I grind my colours from natural materials: I have found a special field whose clay makes this red colour. I feed my cow with mango leaves brought up from Khera; here the altitude is too high for mango trees. Then I collect her urine and dry it in the sun to get this pure yellow. Green is the juice of a special leaf found in the forest. Blue comes from lapis lazuli found in the mountains and white is powdered limestone."

Sarla whispered to Antonia, "Can I buy a painting for Rita? I'll have to borrow the money from you. Shall I ask him if he wants to sell any?"

Antonia whispered back, "These are collector's pieces. One day they'll be very valuable. I'm sure he won't mind being asked; in fact he will be glad because he never goes out to sell his work, but he needs the income."

When Masterji left the room for a few minutes Antonia continued, "His art will die with him, because he has no children. He learned to paint from his father and his father learned it from his father. I don't think his nephew is interested in painting..." she glanced at the door through which the fierce young man had stormed earlier.

From the argument we'd overheard, I suspected Masterji's nephew was involved with the Liberation Front, but I would have to ask any questions later. I was feeling restless and impatient to be on our way.

Sarla bought two paintings, Antonia bought one, Piloo also bought three and Sidhartha chose the one that reminded him of me, to give me as a present.

Masterji took the pile of fifty and one hundred rupee notes without counting them. Piloo said in a respectful way the pictures were far too cheap and wanted to pay more. "There is no need," he replied. Then the painter made neat parcels by placing sheets of clean paper over each painting, placing them in a plastic bag and then tacking it with needle and thread into a piece of clean white cloth. He tied that loosely but firmly with string and bowed as he presented it to Antonia. "God has blessed me today. You like my work and that is enough reward."

I wondered if the nephew would snatch the money from his uncle as soon as we left and run off to the forest.

"Masterji, you are a great artist," Antonia said.

"No. He is the great artist," and Master Nandkishore pointed to the sky. "I am just an instrument in His creation."

We left the house of the artist excited by what we had seen and everyone was talking all at once as we walked back to the rest house.

"As one among thousands and thousands, if not millions, of dancers in this wonderful country I am constantly gobsmacked at the wealth of artistic talent. Most artists – be they painters, poets, potters or musicians – go unnoticed. They learn their art from their parents and practise it quietly all their lives, very often in obscure little villages. They'll never be famous or wealthy, but they don't do their art to become celebrities. It's their birthright and they just exercise it. A gift from God, to be used in his service."

"Sarla," Piloo added, "did you see his prayer

corner? Every time he starts to paint, he prays. All his work is dedicated to God."

"I believe we are all artists, in our own way." Antonia spread her arms wide. Covered by her shawl, she looked like an angel about to fly. "Life has no meaning unless every action is as fine as a work of art…"

I was thinking how lucky I was to have such a teacher and such a friend, when I caught Sarla trying to catch Sidhartha's eye. I knew what she was thinking and I felt irritated.

When we woke up next day we found it had been raining all night. Water was dripping from the broken gutters of the bungalow and the air had turned cold and damp. Chowkidar lit the fire and we ate our breakfast to the sound of thunder and lightning. Travelling was going to be impossible, so we decided to wait it out until the next day.

Twenty-three

❧

SARLA

The rain drummed away on the roof, relentlessly, like it would never end. The fire hardly gave off any heat, so curling up with a book wasn't an option. Piloo found some ancient cards in a drawer, but there were several missing from the pack. We were all feeling bored, and in any case rain always makes me yawn. I remembered the day in our Bayswater kitchen when it had been lashing down and I'd wanted to run away and find another life.

Piloo was beating an impatient tattoo on the cover of her book. She was reading *Fire of Transformation*, with a picture of a handsome young guru on the cover. Inside were pictures of the same guru five years later. He had certainly undergone some transformation. She put it down and pulled her shawl closer.

"Come on, everyone, let's go out and look at the village school."

"Good idea," agreed Sidhartha. "And Bina and I can talk to the local doctor at the clinic."

We opened our big black umbrellas and splashed up the lane into the village, where we parted ways.

The school consisted of a gloomy two-room brick box with a small office for the head teacher. She was busy knitting a candy-coloured cardigan at her desk under a forty-watt bulb, but welcomed us enthusiastically.

The younger children learned their lessons sitting cross-legged on mats in front of a grey blackboard. Their class teacher looked severely at them, addressing them in a loud shrill voice, occasionally hitting one of them with a ruler. She made them answer questions and they responded in dull, singsong voices.

"What is the capital of India?"

"Delhi, Miss."

"What are the names of the five largest rivers? The principle cities? Who is the president of India? How do you say *namaste* in English?" And so on.

"Very hardship post," the teacher told us. "Teaching in village schools is not being interesting. Parents are not having value for education – one minute they are taking children out to look for lost cow, another time they are calling them to take care of baby. Girls are being married at twelve… It is hopeless!"

A man stuck his head into the classroom. "Teacher, our cow has run away. I need Kundan."

She sighed. "You see situation?" Impatiently she nodded to a spindly ten-year-old, who scrambled to his feet and scuttled off.

There were no pictures on the stained and dingy walls, no charts and no maps. In the playground I couldn't see a single piece of equipment, not even a swing. Some children had drawn hopscotch rectangles in the dirt, and one broken goalpost only drew attention to the depressing environment.

"Must be awful going to that school … poor kids."

"The money for their school is probably eaten up by local politicians before it gets to where it's supposed to get to. You can see why people are so fed up in these parts; no wonder they support a movement – even when it's as amateurish as the Liberation Front," Antonia explained. "That's what those boys are aiming at: to be on the side of the peasant, stand up for their rights and get them to start protesting against the whole corrupt system."

Back at the rest house, we had lunch all together at the dining table, pulling on all our extra clothes to keep warm. The school visit had lowered our spirits, but Bina and Sidhartha had come back bubbling with ideas about how they were going to reform the countryside after they qualified.

"It's clarified my ideas," Sidhartha said a little pompously. "I can see the possibilities and I've made up my mind to do research in traditional medicine – you know, using local plants and herbs. You don't always need to prescribe drugs for simple ailments."

Bina's eyes were shining. "The doctor told us that the forests were full of herbs and roots and leaves that can cure many diseases. But he prescribes drugs because the drug companies pay him to and he can't afford to live on his government salary."

"Very honest of him to admit that," remarked Piloo.

"He's a nice man. He told us that American multinationals have taken out patents on local wild plants so they can *sell them back to us*! Isn't it shocking that our government has allowed it?" Bina continued, "Sidhartha and I are going to try and come back here and work for the villagers when we are qualified doctors."

"What a great idea!" chorused Antonia and Piloo.

The romance was obviously taking a serious turn.

Piloo looked fondly at the pair. "I envy you! How wonderful to be starting your life with all your ideals to explore."

I wondered if she missed out on never having been married. I don't remember her ever having had a partner either. Maybe she'd never got over Ashok.

By morning it had stopped raining, but no one knew where Kishenchand had disappeared with his mules.

The chowkidar nodded his head in a meaningful way, "Memsahib, he has been gone for the past two days."

Antonia said severely, "I think you are trying to tell me that Kishenchand has been on a bender. Well, will you please fetch him out of his hooch den and tell him we have to catch the afternoon bus from Khera."

The chowkidar moved his sad little kitchen rag from his right shoulder to his left, nodded vigorously and left to find the truant.

He was back an hour later dragging poor Kishenchand by one ear. "He has been drinking too much," he pronounced to Antonia and Piloo, practically throwing the poor man on the verandah.

The muleteer looked terrible, with puffy bloodshot eyes and grizzly cheeks. He bowed his head and waited like a naughty schoolboy for the reprimand. Antonia was furious because she was worried about our safety and making it to Khera in time to catch the next bus.

We thanked the chowkidar, promising to come again, and took a different route back, which was shorter and didn't have the impressive views we had seen on our way into Rewari.

Antonia grumbled, "I don't know what's happened to the man. A lot of them drink, but this one used to be teetotal. He's been on something more than barley beer for sure."

Bina, Sidhartha and I walked on ahead at a brisk pace, with Piloo and Antonia and the mules behind us. The air was humid and warm after the rain. We took a narrow cart track, soft with leaf mould and mud and quite difficult to manoeuvre in places. It was dark under the canopy of trees, but we saw the sun glinting through the branches. On the left of the track the mountainside was thick with ferns, dog rose and wild raspberries; on the right it fell into a steep ravine. With hardly any gaps in the dense wood there wasn't much to see, which is why Antonia had chosen the other, longer, route the first time. The smells here were also different: damp earth, pine and fungi. The trees dripped like bunged up shower heads and a sudden breeze sent raindrops splattering down on our heads. We heard the friendly cooing of pigeons and mynahs in the woods, but otherwise it was very silent. There wasn't much conversation either.

"Very quiet, isn't it?" We heard Piloo's voice from the back. "Not a soul in sight, no huts or animals or anything. Sarla, come and tell me – did you have a nice time? What are your impressions?"

I fell back to join them. "Where do I start? I've enjoyed every bit of it. It's been such a great trip – thanks, Antonia. Maybe the biggest surprise is how little the village people have, and still they can smile and be so friendly. I'd say they're happier than lots of people who are richer and live in cities with cars and TVs and things."

Piloo couldn't resist adding, "As Guruji says, what is happiness?" She squeezed my arm affectionately. "And I was worried that you'd be homesick and find Daroga wouldn't be up to scratch."

I chatted with the aunties, letting Bina and Sidhartha carry on ahead. After a while, with all the bends in the path, we lost sight of them, but could hear them murmuring in front. Kishenchand was lagging quite far behind, his mules clop-clopping slowly and sadly like their master. When next we caught up with the lovebirds, they were standing still, hand in hand, looking left up into the wooded slope of the mountain. Probably a bird or squirrel or something, I thought, but when we caught up and were able to follow the direction of their gaze we saw it was fixed on a boy. He was standing on a large boulder, about halfway up the hill, shouting down to us and waving his arms. It looked as though he was signalling for help.

"Shall I go and see what he wants? Maybe he's hurt himself, or maybe someone up there needs help." Sidhartha was ready to scramble up, when on an impulse I offered to go with him. "I'll come too, in case you need something from the luggage – I could come back for it." I knew he'd brought a first aid kit with him.

"Sarla, there's no need…" Piloo said. "Sidhartha can manage. It'll be slippery and dangerous going up."

But I was already climbing, only a few steps behind Sidhartha. "I think I recognize that boy," I puffed. We were closer to the boulder now. "He was called away from his class to look for a runaway cow." It was the same boy all right and I remembered his name: Kundan. "Hi, Kundan," I shouted. "What's the problem?"

I knew he wouldn't understand me, but wanted

him to know that we were coming to help. Maybe the cow had fallen into a gully, or his dad had broken a leg. The boy kept beckoning and kept on climbing higher, to a point where the path below and the others went out of our sight. We rounded an escarpment, trudging still higher. Sidhartha stopped to wipe the sweat off his face and that was the last thing I saw.

Suddenly, in one swoop, darkness descended and I'd been blinded. I couldn't see anything, and I couldn't breathe. It took a few seconds to realize that something had been put over my head – something like a scratchy cloth – and someone's hand was clamped firmly over the cloth, covering my mouth, so I wouldn't shout or be heard at all.

From the scrabbling and grunting near me I guessed the same thing had happened to Sidhartha. Then I was being half pushed and half carried for at least another ten minutes, until we were forced suddenly to stop. The cover was lifted off over my head and I saw it was a gunny bag in which you store rice. It was dusty and scratchy, and I started to sneeze. Then I felt my wrists being tied behind me so tightly that I yelped.

"Don't be so rough!" Sidhartha snapped at the men who had surrounded us. There were four of them, all wearing khakis and army boots. They had guns strapped to their backs, and scarves round their faces. Their eyes glinted through the woollen masks.

"*Chup*! Quiet!" a muffled voice spoke through the face covering. We were pushed to the ground, while they towered over us pointing their guns. I remember thinking, this is like the movies, it cannot be real. We had been shoved inside a stone hut with one small window and a couple of string beds against two walls. They kept pushing until we were sitting with our backs against a wall, on the dirt floor.

"Who are you? What are you going to do with us?" I guessed these were the kinds of questions Sidhartha was asking. I couldn't follow anything they said, except the words "Liberation Front". One of them curtly gave Sidhartha permission to tell me what was happening.

Sidhartha explained, "We've been kidnapped. They're going to keep us here and then go down and demand money from Antonia and Piloo. He says they won't hurt us as long as they get the money they need."

"Otherwise?" My heart fell into my shoes because I knew the aunties weren't carrying a lot of cash with them.

"Otherwise, I don't know. They're not dangerous,

Sarla, just desperate. I think we're their last resort."

It was all very well for him to be so rational, but I was terrified. Those guns looked very real to me and the men didn't seem to be exactly sensitive souls. I needed to pee and I was very thirsty. The hut smelled of unwashed bodies and cheap cigarettes. The only cheering thought was that no one, absolutely *no one*, had been kidnapped in my school and this was going to make a terrific story when I got back – if I ever did.

Twenty-four

❧

BINA

We had been in our own world, chatting about this and that; we described members of our families, our friends and how we would reach out to those who needed our help once we became doctors. I found Sidhartha had such a lot of understanding and sympathy for poor people. He was everything I could have hoped for, so when he started up the hillside I was upset that our time together had been interrupted. Then, when Sarla followed him in her usual impulsive way, I felt very uneasy; we were supposed to be hurrying back for the afternoon bus and my feeling was that Sarla and Sidhartha were taking a silly risk. A minute later and they were both out of our sight.

Something strange was happening to Kishenchand. He was squatting by the edge of the road with his head in his hands, groaning and muttering to himself.

When I asked him, "What's the matter?" he looked up, and his unshaven face was miserable as if his granny had died. "Are you feeling worse?"

"No, *behanji*, no," and he hid his face in his arms, not wanting to talk, so I went back to Piloo and Antonia.

I found them leaning peacefully against a rock waiting for Sidhartha and Sarla to come back from their mission of mercy. They were shelling peanuts and Antonia offered me a handful. "Hope they won't be too long," she commented. Meanwhile, we heard retching noises as Kishenchand emptied the contents of his stomach over the side of the precipice.

"Stupid man," Piloo said without pity.

Half an hour went by and there was still no sign of those two. "Something must be wrong. Why are they taking so long?" Antonia got up, stretching her arms over her head. "We really must make a move."

Just then we heard gunshots, one after the other, *crack-crack-crack-crack*. They came from beyond the hill that Sarla and Sidhartha had climbed. Echoes bounced off the hillside and a great crowd of mountain crows rose up from the pine trees, cawing and squawking: *"Caw-caw-caw-caw."* It was such an eerie sound it sent shivers down my spine.

"Oh my God!" we all said, terrified for Sarla and Sidhartha, and frightened for ourselves.

There was another round of shots and then absolute, deathly silence. I saw a brown monkey nervously looking down from a tree, twitching its tail.

"Kishenchand! What is happening? Do you know anything about this?" Antonia went to him and shook his shoulder.

"Sorry, memsahib, sorry. I didn't know they were going to kill the children."

"Are you talking about Sidhartha and Sarla? Kill them? What nonsense is this?"

I swear, at this point my heart froze.

Piloo stood over the mule man. "You knew what was going to happen? Are you talking about the Liberation Front boys? Did they do something to you? Is that why you're drunk?"

She had guessed correctly. "Sorry, memsahib, sorry. They said they would hurt my own children. It's that Manoj and his friends. We thought they were good boys, but they have gone to the bad. I should have told you before, but they said they just wanted money for the kidnapping – they said nothing about hurting the Baba and Baby." He broke into deep sobs.

"You were blackmailed to keep quiet? And I thought I could trust you!" Antonia was disgusted. Standing very still, she cupped her ear with her hand. "I can hear something – listen." Faintly we caught what might have been the noise of snapping branches. The crackling grew louder and we looked nervously at one another. Someone was coming down the mountain.

"Sidhartha! Sarla!" I screamed, wanting to rush up the hill, although I couldn't see anyone still.

Antonia held me firmly in her arms. "Ssh, stay calm. Wait."

It wasn't Sidhartha and Sarla but three men, dressed like soldiers, leaping down the slope from rock to rock, nimble as mountain goats. We couldn't make out their faces but they were pointing guns at us. Piloo had been trained to deal with difficult people in her job. She spoke calmly. "Where are the boy and the girl? Have you got them?"

The leader of the gang came up closer, still pointing his gun. His voice was muffled because of the scarf round his face. "Yes, we have them. They will not be released until you pay us one lakh rupees."

Antonia laughed sarcastically. "Do you really think we are carrying that kind of money?"

"What do you have with you? Jewellery? Watches? Show me!"

"Huh, they have paintings with them worth a fortune," another man said.

How did he know that? Could he be the angry young man who'd pushed his way past us when we were waiting by Masterji's staircase? Masterji had mentioned a nephew. Was this scruffy looking bandit that same person?

The leader pushed him aside. "Idiot! Imbecile! Shut up and let me do the talking." He prodded Antonia with his gun. "Show me what you have. Take off your gold chain. Now your watch, and that ring."

"It was my mother's. She's dead, and I'm certainly not giving it to you."

The man moved to slap her face, when I burst out angrily, "*Badtameez!* How dare you! She is my teacher, my guru. Don't you dare touch her! Who are you anyway, to demand our things and to kidnap our friends?"

I was so furious that I could have punched him, gun or no gun.

He lowered his scarf a little so we could hear him clearly. "My name is Sadhuram. I am the acting chief of the Liberation Front. I am the son of the famous bandit Beharilal, the partner of Shobharani. She is our Devi and we are fighting with her against injustice and for the rights of the poor."

I could hardly believe what I heard. Sadhuram, who had known my mother as a small boy. Sadhuram, who had seen his father die before his own eyes! Sadhuram, whose life was so closely linked to mine! I responded instinctively.

"And do you know me? Do you know who I am? I am the only daughter of Shobharani. I am the daughter of your Devi, the Devi that you boast about. She is my mother and I demand that you let your prisoners go!"

I could tell that everyone had stopped breathing. At that moment it seemed even the leaves on the trees and bushes stilled their lonely rustling.

Sadhuram sneered. "Rubbish! You're lying. That's impossible! Shobharani's daughter lives in Daroga. What are you doing here? She wouldn't be wandering all over the mountains with these people!"

"These people, as you call them, are my dearest friends. You know nothing about us, you stupid man. My name is Bina, the granddaughter of Havildar Hiralal. Ask anyone!"

"You, the Devi's daughter?" He tore off his scarf. "How can you prove it? Show me proof!"

I unclasped my gold locket, flipped it open with my nail and let him see the photo of my mother. He looked long and hard at the image.

"How old were you when she left your father?"

"Two."

"Which village did your parents live in?"

I told him.

He quizzed me in detail about my family, about my mother, until he was satisfied. I saw his expression softening; he looked at me and then at the others and then everything changed.

"Is it true?" he demanded. He asked Antonia, "Is she the Devi's child?"

"Every word is true."

His face became full of humility and shame, where minutes before there had been nothing but cold arrogance.

"Sorry. *Sorry, sorry, sorry.*" He threw down his gun, folded his hands and knelt down before me, bowing his head as if he were saying his prayers.

"Forgive me. I did not know; forgive my ignorance." And he turned round to order the other men to fetch Sarla and Sidhartha. "Forgive me, sister. Shame overcomes me," he kept saying. "You are my sister because our parents loved each other. Fate has brought about this meeting. I wasn't to know ... how was I to know?"

His confusion only made my heart beat faster, and I started to cry. I was so relieved and so grateful. For the second time my mother had saved the situation. I wanted to touch Sadhuram, and even embrace him, but I restrained myself. Instead I went and flung myself in Antonia's arms. She held me tight and let me cry my heart out.

Twenty minutes or so later we heard cheerful voices and there were Sidhartha and Sarla, running to us, shouting and laughing with relief.

We had missed the bus, so we decided to return to Rewari for another night. The Liberation Front boys accompanied us all the way and spent the night on the verandah floor, under blankets loaned by the chowkidar. They were very helpful and washed up the pots and pans in the kitchen before settling down in front of the fire with the five of us. We were fascinated by their story and couldn't hear enough about their lives and experiences.

Sadhuram told it from the beginning, when his papa met up with my mother, how the gang was formed, what they did and the life they led. We heard about the times he had been their courier and messenger. He had worshipped my mother! He talked about her strong leadership – how she was so brave, fearless and fair to all. He spoke about how he had learned about injustice and how the system had no pity for the poor. Last of all he told us about the terrible day when the police overcame the gang and shot his father dead. He remembered it in great detail. "I dream about that night very often."

Then he explained their desperation after the failure of the arms drop, and the arrest of Prof.

I was feeling a mixture of pity and helplessness towards my adopted new brother. "What can I do for you?" I asked.

He shrugged. "We can only help ourselves," he said realistically. "But please don't think bad things about us. If only more people like you would understand why we are so angry, everything would be different. But the people, the high-ups, don't remember those who have nothing. Our villagers are so neglected and there is no one to speak up for them."

Sarla had sat as quiet as a mouse drinking it all in, but then she spoke up in her bossy way, "Manoj, you have to go and say sorry to your uncle, Master Nandkishore. Promise me you'll never shout at him again. His paintings are his work and he can do what he likes with his own work. Why should he hand over his money to you?"

Manoj wouldn't look at her. He stared at the carpet. "We were desperate for food."

Antonia and Piloo exchanged glances. "We could get in terrible trouble with the police if they find out, but take this," and they handed over all their spare cash to Sadhuram.

Sidhartha also emptied his wallet and then, with

great seriousness, he made a promise. "After I finish my training as a doctor, I am coming back to this area to work with the people."

I nodded in agreement. "And me – you can count on me too."

Sadhuram cleared his throat – he smoked awful, cheap cigarettes – but even though Antonia and Piloo had asked him to smoke outside, I could smell them every time he opened his mouth.

"Let me tell you another story about my family. It's not an unusual one. After my father was killed, the police came and beat up my mother, though she had never done anything wrong – just sent food and medicines to the gang. They broke two of her ribs and a finger. She was a beautiful woman and so was my older sister and now they had no protection. Both of them were raped by the local thakur, the rich landlord. No one in the village wanted to have anything to do with them after that. Luckily, my uncle, her brother, had been depositing the money sent by my father in a bank account – it was obviously money they had robbed from the rich. He came to fetch us and took us back to his home in Ambala. That's how I got an education and how my sister was able to get married. My mother, God bless her, died at the age of forty-five.

"That thakur made a business of sending his men

out to buy little girls – ten-year-olds, twelve-year-olds – and he'd then sell them on to brothel keepers in Delhi and Bombay. When a man died, the thakur would grab his land and turn out the family. If someone owed him money, he would have him killed. If a lower caste person drew water from one of his wells, he would strip them naked, parade them around the village and have them whipped. I grew up with all this injustice: an everyday occurrence. When I met Prof I was more than ready to change the world.

"Ask the boys, ask Manoj and Dhiraj and Tiny: is mine a fictional tale? They will tell you no; it happens all the time; it's happening today."

For a long time we were all very quiet. The logs smouldered until there was only a faint glow and then the electricity suddenly went.

"Bed, match and candle," said Antonia yawning widely. "We are all exhausted and we still have a long march tomorrow. Are you coming with us to Khera?"

"Yes, Aunty," Sadhuram replied. "Until the outskirts of the village. We will walk there with you."

We fell into our beds, blew out the candles and slept soundly.

We were up by eight for our porridge and toast. For the second time in twenty-four hours we took the shorter route to Khera. It was an uneventful journey and we arrived in good time for the bus.

Sadhuram pleaded, "Don't forget us. And, Bina-didi, go and see your mother and tell her you have found your brother. Somehow I will try and meet up with you at Rakhi time; you can tie the thread round my wrist, like all sisters do at the festival and I will give you a present. You are my sister and I promise to always take care of you. Look after your mother's needs, and remind her she is still our Devi and the people are waiting for her guidance."

I was so happy because I'd never had a brother on whose wrist I could tie a Rakhi thread, who would promise to protect me. Now I had Sadhuram.

And I had my mother – my poor, extraordinary, brave, foolish, reckless, strong, now helpless mother; helpless for herself, but not for me. My mother, who somehow rose from behind her grim prison walls to reach out to the daughter who called for her when she needed help. Maybe now was the time for me to reach out to her.

Twenty-five

🐾

SARLA

It was rattle and roll once again, all the way back to Daroga on the afternoon bus, but somehow we managed to sleep through the noise and movement; we were too tired even to make small talk, or admire the scenery. The excitement of the last two days – listening to Sadhuram and his friends, plus miles of walking – had finished me off.

The taxi brought us back to Stoneleigh by eight thirty, just in time for dinner. Sidhartha was going to eat with us and afterwards his chauffeur would take him and Antonia home.

I felt an enormous sense of relief as I lugged my rucksack up the verandah steps. The familiar sight of dear old Carmen lumbering to her feet to lick my hand was so comforting. It was nice to imagine that she'd been waiting, her chin on her paws, for us. The house was bright with lights and I knew the fire would be lit. I opened the front door and, to my utter amazement, who did I see but *my mother*, standing by the fireplace with her arms open to welcome me.

We hugged and hugged. Under my hands I felt her frame, like chicken bones. "Why are you so scrawny?"

"Why are you so much taller?" she asked. "It's only been six weeks. Oh, I see you're thinner!" She held me out to take a good look.

"Not as thin as you, Ma. What have you been up to?"

She had aged by ten years. I saw lines I hadn't noticed before, and apart from the grey shadows there was something in her eyes I didn't recognize, something wounded and sad. She had always had such bounce, but she appeared to be walking on eggshells. "I haven't been too well," she explained abruptly. "I'll be all right again once I get some rest and sleep."

Nani signalled from the other side, *Don't ask questions.*

I had never seen Rita in such a state before; I was really worried. What did she mean by she wasn't well?

I managed to get Nani in the kitchen. "What's wrong?" I whispered.

"She's taken sick leave – exhaustion, you know. She's been through a tough time, but I'm sure she'll tell you everything once she's rested. Be cheerful and let's all take good care of her. Try not to ask her too many questions tonight: she just came in from Delhi this morning." I tried to read more in Nani's face, but she hurried away to see if dinner was ready.

We had decided, we five travellers, not to say anything about Sadhuram and the gang. It would have been too complicated and could have put my grandparents in a difficult position with their friend Mr Chowdhry, the ex-police commissioner.

But there were many other things to talk about – our journey there, the naked sadhu, Forest Rest House and the chowkidar, the commodes, the school and the clinic; and, most importantly, our afternoon with Masterji.

I gave Rita her painting. She took it without enthusiasm, thanking me in a listless voice. A dread, that Nani hadn't told the whole truth, came back. I wanted to shout at my mother, "What is going on? Why are you behaving so oddly?" But I took a deep breath and tried to steady myself. After all, whatever it was couldn't be hidden for ever.

Instead I concentrated on enjoying every mouthful of Hira's delicious food, to make up for the starvation rations we'd been having. Piloo had forgotten to pack chocolate and all there had been for peckish moments were boring Glaxo biscuits. This evening Hira had outdone himself.

"That chowkidar can only make rice and dal," I informed Nani with a mouth full of *keema mutter*.

"And powdered custard," added Sidhartha.

After dinner was over he said, "Let's meet up tomorrow," remembering, in time, to stop himself from hugging Bina in front of her grandparents.

Rita's eyes were closing so I couldn't say much to her after dinner, but so were mine. We called it a day and went to bed.

At breakfast I looked carefully to see if Rita had lightened up.

"Couldn't sleep," she answered, when I asked how she was feeling.

The phone rang, too loudly for the sombre atmosphere at breakfast; it was Sidhartha asking if he could come over at lunchtime. Bina had to go back to school in a couple of days so I guessed he wanted to see her as much as possible.

"Yes, of course, you know you're welcome – come to lunch."

"No, no," hissed my mother. "Not today, please, Poochi. I need to talk about something with you.

Maybe he could come later this evening..."

My heart turned over. Something told me this was serious; maybe my mother had multiple sclerosis, or cancer or motor neurone disease.

I ate my French toast and honey and waited for her to finish her tea. She always had at least four cups in the morning. I wanted to tell her to hurry up, but remembered Nani's warning about being gentle with her, so I waited till she was ready. At last she was through. She yawned and stretched and stumbled to her feet, almost knocking over her chair.

"I think I'll have a bath first," she said, walking in her new slow-motion way to the spare room. "I'll call you when I'm done."

"How's Des?" I managed to put in, trying desperately to sound normal.

"OK, I suppose. Must ring him this afternoon. Will you remind me?"

Weirder and weirder; where were all her usual gushy exclamations and girlish squeals?

At last she came out of the bathroom, towelling her long hair, taking puffs from a cigarette as she did her make-up. I stopped myself from making any comment.

She settled down on her unmade bed, cross-legged, and looking like death warmed up, even though she'd put on a little war paint. "Come," she patted the blanket. "Come and sit near me."

I obeyed, feeling leaden and wobbly at the same time. Then I couldn't help myself any more and burst out, "Mum, what is going on? Are you all right? Are you trying to tell me you're ill? You're not going to die, are you? Are you?" I reached for her hand.

She laughed weakly, wheezing a little. "Oh, trust you, Poochi! Not at all – certainly not – you don't get rid of me that easily." She paused. "Sorry, darling, I'm being awful but I have some news that is going to blow your mind: I've been trying to get up the courage to tell you. It's a long story, so be patient."

She sat thinking, as if she was trying to gather up the words and phrases she needed. Finally, after what seemed like ages but was probably only three or four minutes, she began.

"Once, there was a young girl called Lila – yes the same one – who arrived at Captain and Mrs Sehgal's – yes, Nana and Nani's – house in Meerut cantonment with her brand new husband, Hiralal Chaubey. Hira was a strapping young Pahari from the hills and held the position of orderly to the young captain. He was a fine man but quick to blow a fuse and very stubborn even then. The newlyweds were happy and she smiled all the time, wearing her new bridal clothes and jewellery and looking forward to the son they would have one day. But the son never came; instead some years later they had a daughter, with difficulty and many complications. The baby's name, as you know, was Shobharani, Shobha for short.

"Lila was an emotional young girl, easily moved to tears, anxious and nervous in temperament. From time to time she would lapse into a ..." (here Rita searched for the right word) "depression. Maybe it was postnatal, maybe she worried that the boy they wanted would never come; so Nani started giving her little jobs in the house – some ironing, some mending and dusting. This gave her something to do and the child could play around her safely. Hira and Lila moved from one army posting to another with Nana and Nani, but no more children came.

"Then there was a huge political upset in India. We went to war against China in 1961 over a few useless bits of mountain desert. It was a boundary dispute, but China quickly forgot all the friendship treaties (*Hindi-Chini bhai-bhai*: India and China are brothers was a popular slogan) and invaded Indian territory. Nana was now a brigadier and he went off with the army to fight, taking his batman Hira with him.

"Now, the irony was that as soon as Hira had gone, Lila found she was pregnant and she was certain it was a boy, because she had done a pilgrimage to a sacred mountain to pray for a boy.

"Many months later Nana returned home, hair peppered with grey, frostbite in his toes, but without Hira. Hira had been captured by the Chinese and no one knew his whereabouts. He might have been a prisoner of war, or his body could be under an avalanche in the high Himalaya.

"Nine months after Hira left, the baby that Lila was expecting turned out to be another daughter and Lila became very ill. She cursed the fate that had left her to bring up two girls on her own, without a man. Time passed, without any news of Hira, and in the meantime a relative from Lila's village arrived with a marriage proposal for Shobha, who was now fourteen.

"Lila was beside herself with worry and nerves. The baby was sickly, because her milk had dried up, and she felt Shobha would be a burden until she went to her own home to become someone else's responsibility. Lila was in no mood to listen to advice from Nana and Nani, who begged her to let Shobha finish her schooling. At least she should find out more about the boy and the family to which he belonged. Were they decent people? Would they take good care of Shobha? The little baby had now turned two.

"In the end Shobha was married and left her mother's house for good; but imagine, just weeks after she'd gone to her new home, who should turn up but Hira! He was skin and bones, but at least he was alive. He came back home to a wife and a two-year-old baby girl, and the news that his older daughter was married and gone to her in-laws' home.

"Hira had been tortured by the Chinese, so he was in a shocking state of mental and physical health. He had changed from a loving husband to a jealous and vengeful tyrant. He accused his wife of being unfaithful and having a baby that was not his. How could it have happened after eleven years of being barren?

"His brutal reaction tipped Lila completely over the edge and she had to be hospitalized. What was going to happen to the little girl now? There was only one solution. Nana and Nani had one daughter of their own, Piloo, so they decided to adopt the unwanted baby. There was only one condition: that the child would never be told about her natural parents."

At this point Ma stopped for breath. She got off the bed and walked around the room. She looked out of the window at the misty blue mountains. She poured herself a glass of water. She fiddled with her damp hair, twisting it into a chignon. Then she came back and sat down again and watched me. Her story must have moved things in my mind and made me more open to possibilities. In a way, nothing would have shocked me now; I had been prepared, so to speak, for whichever twist or turn the rest of the tale would take. And yet, it could only go in one particular direction – towards the fate of the baby that had been adopted by Nana and Nani.

"What happened to the baby?" I asked very quietly. She didn't say anything. "Ma, the baby? Ma, wait. I think I know. Were you the baby that was adopted?"

She looked long and hard at me. A vein throbbed in her temple, her eyes filled with tears and she nodded.

How could that be possible? Lila and Hira were my actual grandparents, Bina was my cousin and the Bandit Queen of the Hills was my aunt? In that great rush of new information that flooded my head and then my consciousness, I was aware only of my mother weeping silently. I gently wrapped her in my arms and hushed her. I stroked her hair and told her how much I loved her and how glad I was that she'd shared this with me. I knew I had to be in charge now and humour was the only weapon I could use against her anguish.

"Shhh, shhh," I cradled her. "I don't know if I can cope with two sets of grandparents, an extra aunt who's in the lock-up and a cousin who's fallen in *lurve* with a maharajah's grandson. Look, Mum, all I ever wanted was a *normal* family. This is too complicated!"

She sniffed and smiled a little. Drying her eyes on her sleeve she asked, "Do I have your permission to have a fag?"

"No. You can't take advantage of the situation to indulge your vices. Just tell me one thing – how long have you known all this, and why didn't you tell me before?"

"I found out by accident during that famous visit six years ago. I was looking through some old family files and I chanced upon the adoption papers. You can imagine what a huge shock it was. I wanted to tell you right away, but Nana wouldn't let me. He said at eight you were too young and needed stability, so we had a flaming row and I left with you the next day. I was incensed! I couldn't come to terms with the fact that my real parents (who, after all, had rejected me) were in daily contact with my adopted parents. It took ages to come to terms with the fact that Piloo wasn't my real sister, that my parents worked as domestic servants for Nana and Nani, that I wasn't the person I thought I was.

"Then there was all the other business of my sister Shobha, mentally ill and in jail for life. I think I hated Nana and Nani for everything they stood for – their comfortable middle-class life, their desperation not to change anything – I just didn't want anything to do with them. I know it was selfish: and I should have gone for professional help to sort out my head, but I was too busy with work. It was just easier to stay away and keep you away from them. Of course, at the time I thought it was Nana and Nani who were selfish: they didn't want their carefully constructed world to come apart; they were too old to have such a big change in their lives. But here we are. It's all come apart and we have to bring it together somehow."

My head was throbbing now. I lay back and looked up at the ceiling. A little while ago I'd thought that, give or take a few details, I was a fairly "normal" person (except for not being part of a conventional family) and now the wheel had turned. I was part of a most bizarre family situation.

It was lunchtime, but we had been tactfully left alone. Lunch would have been kept warm for us.

"What's going to happen now? What are we going to do?"

"Let me tell you what I've decided for myself," my mother said. "I am taking sick leave (no, Poochi, I haven't got cancer or MS or any of those diseases you've come up with). I am very tired. I've seen too much killing in Tarekstan and I can't handle any more orphaned children, raped women and dead soldiers. I am going to stay in India for a while. I need a very long break. Maybe, when I'm stronger I'll write a book about my sister. About her and all the women who have suffered like her…"

"You'll want to meet Sadhuram then," I interrupted.

"Sadhuram? Who's he? No, tell me later." She waved a hand to stop me going on. "But you have a choice. You can stay on here and go to school at the convent, or you can go back to school in London. Grania's parents will have you to stay with them during term-time, I've talked to them already. In the end it's what you feel comfortable with."

Now this really was a grown-up decision. I needed time to think, but right now I had cramps in my legs. "Come on, Mum – let's have some lunch, I'm starving."

Rita managed a little laugh – a genuine one this time – and went to splash water on her face. It was *almost* like old times again.

I didn't know what I should do. Firstly, I didn't

like Hira, even if he did happen to be my grand-father. Lila was no problem; I'd felt warmly towards her from the beginning – we had our little games and jokes. But I would never get over the mean streak I'd witnessed in Hira: his attitude to girls, to his wife, to his daughter Shobha, to his grand-daughter Bina. I was going to find it hard to forgive his insensitivity, for not listening, or understanding, and being so inflexible. But then, I reckoned, Nana was the grandfather I'd always known and loved. I didn't have to switch loyalties just because he wasn't Rita's real father. I remembered his many kindnesses: his gentleness and patience with Bina, his generosity, his perfect manners and his affection to me. I decided I'd stay with Nana as my grand-father.

Then there was the other, very grown-up, deci-sion about whether I should go back or stay on. Here was the opportunity I'd dreamed about: to be part of Grania's family. But then what about Bina? And Sidhartha? I wanted to be a part of their lives too. I loved my school in London and I loved everything about London, even the rain, even when it dripped through the privet hedges on my walk home from the bus stop. I loved school dinners and drama club and my class. All the girls had been together since we were nine. In the coming term we were going to have a really fun young form teacher, who was a bit hippy and wrote poetry. I'd miss all that if I stayed.

I went into the garden where Bholuram was deadheading the dahlias. On the grass a crow looked at me with a cheeky glint in its eye. Its wings had an extra sheen that I hadn't seen in English crows – purply green – and its black feathers were blacker than anything else in nature. In my head I suddenly heard the cawing of crows when the shotguns had gone off; how they rose like cinders from the trees in the forest. I thought of my aunt Shobharani's song – *the crows are your brothers, the kite is your sister-in-law* – and I thought, maybe my roots are here.

All of a sudden I longed to tell Bina and Sidhartha what had happened, and I was dying to tell Bina that we were cousins. As I passed Bholuram he gave me his sweet toothless smile and I said "namaste ji" to him. I wasn't so bad at languages, I thought. I'll learn Hindi and then I can talk to everyone.

I went inside to phone Sidhartha to ask him over for tea.

Twenty-six

❧

BINA

Thirteen years later

"Mamamamama…" Holding the bars of her play-pen Paro blows a bubble and smiles her irresistible smile, causing her grey eyes to disappear into her fat cheeks.

I make approving noises. "Good girl, clever girl! *Mama*: say, *Mama!*"

We gave her a popular hill name – Parvati, Paro, the wife of the lord of the mountains, Shiva. Her full name is Parvati, and this afternoon her Aunty Sarla is coming from London to stay with us.

She will take the same bus route we took all those years ago. First from Daroga to Khera, then a long hike from there to Rewari. Kishenchand will bring the luggage on Balu (Bhanu died last year) and I will meet my cousin's boyfriend, Sam, for the first time. Sarla says I mustn't be shocked by his red hair – red as carrot halvah, she says. Kishenchand is very familiar with the way to the doctor's house on the other side of the village. It's a lovely little cottage, a wedding present from Princess Vidya. It's made of stone and wood painted blue, like the other village buildings, but we have a proper bathroom upstairs and a little garden for Paro to play in.

Up to the time she was born, I worked in the clinic with my husband every day, but until Paro is at least two years old I will look after her myself. She is so sunny: adorable, beautiful. "Edible," as her father says, and I know Sarla is going to fall in love with her!

I catch the sound of voices in the lane and know they've arrived. I pick up Paro and walk to the gate to meet them. Sarla is wearing a big straw hat, the sun being very strong in July. She throws the hat like a Frisbee over the fence and runs to hold me and the baby in an embrace. She buries her face in Paro's fat little body and breathes in her baby smell. "Mmmmmm."

She looks at me approvingly. "You look incredibly well, Bina. This is Sam, whom you've heard so much about. Sam, my cousin Bina, whom *you've* heard endless stories about."

We go inside, laughing and talking and interrupting one another. After they've dumped their luggage and had a wash, we sit down to tea on the verandah. Paro sits on Sarla's lap playing with a new toy.

We haven't seen one another since Uncleji's funeral last year. Since then Sarla has been writing up her social anthropology thesis on "Popular Medicine in the Eastern Foothills of the Himalaya". She has come for another few months of fieldwork, so we will have lots of time to catch up with one another's lives.

"How is Koshy Aunty?" is one of my first questions. After Uncleji's passing away, Auntyji has lived with Piloo in London.

"Not too bad. Piloo and she are getting along very well together. They've decided not to sell Stoneleigh because real estate is going up and up every year – especially in the hills – and Piloo wants to eventually come back to India and retire in Daroga."

"What does Auntyji do all day in London?"

"She sees Rita at least once a week, she shops for food, goes to concerts and museums, reads, does her tapestry. She misses Nana a lot, but in general she's quite happy."

"And Rita?"

"Busy writing her books and travelling. Des and she have plenty of money, so they lead a very luxe life style. They've just bought a house in Morocco! They're invited everywhere and they're always rushing around … but Mum's latest passion is saving forests in India. She made a film about sustainable forestry that was shown on Channel Four just last week."

We talk about Grandfather and Grandmother, now retired. They live in Stoneleigh and take care of the house for Koshy Aunty. Bholuram also died, so now there is a new gardener and Grandfather drives Uncleji's car. My grandparents come and see Paro quite often, driving up to Khera, continuing by mule to Rewari, laden with presents of vegetables and pickles and biscuits and all the things we can't buy in the village. Grandfather loves playing with the baby and never loses his temper any more.

Antonia is still living in The Nook, with all her animals. She gives dance lessons at the convent and insisted on putting Paro's name on the waiting list, even though I wasn't sure about it.

"You'll kick yourself afterwards if you don't, Bina. Anyway, we have to keep up traditions."

Sam is listening patiently to our excited conversation. I want to make him feel welcome. He is a photographer and is going to do a photo feature on my mother. In spite of Rita's book and all the publicity that brought, Shobharani has not been released from jail. Her mental condition is more or less stable, but she hasn't been pardoned. We are hoping that Sam's pictures and article about the jail will make even more people aware of her story.

I haven't taken Paro to meet her yet. I hesitate because I remember how I felt when I visited the jail as a child. I worry that the oppressive atmosphere will somehow infect her. Sarla says she will come with me this time, and that's sure to give me courage. Before Paro was born I did go once or twice, as Sadhuram had asked me to, but I found it unbearably difficult. My mother didn't know me and I hated to see such suffering. I think about her with feelings of love and concern and I made my peace with her all those years ago.

When I graduated from medical college I sent pictures of the ceremony; also of my wedding and Paro, when she was born. Rita is still trying to get permission for a specialist from Delhi to diagnose her illness and prescribe better medication. Maybe that will help. Maybe she'll be allowed to see a therapist. We keep on hoping.

Sadhuram disappeared for a few years. We heard he'd gone to train with the Maoists in Nepal. Then we heard he was hiding in one of the southern states. Now the rumour is that he is back in our area. The Liberation Front broke up and faded away because

Prof, their leader, was given a long imprisonment. I think he's still serving his term.

Manoj apologized to Master Nandkishore the painter and made friends with him. He now looks after his old uncle in the village. Manoj gives us news of Sadhuram and maybe he'll suddenly appear at our doorstep, but he is still wanted by the police. When the festival comes I shall still tie a Rakhi on his wrist, because I am his adopted sister.

My mobile rings twice. It's our usual signal that my husband is on his way. Then I hear him whistling a tune below the house.

"Listen, Sarla, it's Sidhartha!"

Minutes later he is pushing open the gate, a big smile on his face, walking quickly up the path to greet Sarla, Sam and his baby daughter.

"Dinkoo!" Sarla cries. It's their little joke. "Doctor Sahib! Daddy!" We all laugh and Paro laughs too.

Our hearts are so full that we couldn't fit in any more happiness if we tried.